SAXON'S GHOST

by Steve Fisher

I WAKE UP SCREAMING

DESTINATION TOKYO

WINTER KILL

THE SHELTERING NIGHT

GIVEAWAY

TAKE ALL YOU CAN GET

NO HOUSE LIMIT

IMAGE OF HELL

SAXON'S GHOST

Steve Fisher

SHERBOURNE PRESS, INC.   LOS ANGELES

Library of Congress Catalog Card Number 76–83559
Manufactured in the United States of America by
Kingsport Press, Inc.,
Kingsport, Tenn.

First Printing

For Marilyn

I

IT WAS ONE of the small houses, four hundred seats, small theaters were the only kind that booked him in the big cities any more, and for a magician whose act comprised the entire evening of entertainment, the real magic was any booking at all; even for The Great Saxon, acknowledged not just by press notices and advertisements but other professionals in his trade as the world's foremost sorcerer in the art of legerdemain.

A small, old legitimate playhouse with a dusty-rose, faded brick front on a narrow, cobbled Boston street, the edifice illuminated by glass-enclosed gaslight flickering yellowly, eerily, against a flurry of softly falling snow. It could have been the Eden Theatre in Paris in the 1870s when Hermann the Great performed his Vanity Fair illusion before a dazzling, smartly dressed, properly amazed and appreciative audience that rose applauding wildly when he vanished Mrs. Hermann into her large makeup mirror. Saxon supplied the gaslight torches himself, carrying them with his other props, because that was the aura of illusion he wanted. Those days when magic was revered as great art.

2

The program announcement posted outside the theater did not proclaim him a magician, that was a common, passé word now: you expected a clumsy clown charade—the man in coat-tails deliberately bungling simple sleight-of-hand tricks as if by accident to get people to laugh at him. Saxon didn't care to be laughed at. He had lately even dropped the "Great" from his billing, for it was another old-fashioned cliché. With quiet dignity, the poster read simply:

TONIGHT AT 8:30
AN EVENING WITH
JOSEPH P. SAXON
PERFORMING SUPERNATURAL ACTS
OF BLACK MAGIC

That was the only come-on to get an audience. The public had long ago tired of levitation—a pretty young thing lying suspended in mid-air against a black velvet curtain. Tattling editors had published articles explaining how the trick was done, while movies and night clubs staled to death the sawing of a woman in half. That, too, for him at least, was in discard. A girl disappearing from a cabinet or lying in a wicker basket while swords are thrust into it, the Hindu rope trick, no matter how well done, rabbits popping out of a top hat, playing cards that vanish into thin air, a pitcher of clear water that when poured changes colors, all and other feats like it were hoary.

Ah, but the supernatural. Without encroaching on fraudulent mediums with their shoddy card table seances, the "trance" they pretended to go into, croaking out messages from dearly departed loved ones; without so much as commenting on that breed of charlatans or stooping to duplicate their cheap parlor trick of misty ghost images, floating trumpets, or any of that other paraphernalia, he smoothly presented his own world of "those from beyond," and it intrigued foolish, superstitious, middle-aged women who simply, because they had nothing else left in their empty lives, embraced the occult, and would brave snow and wet streets, paying seven dollars a ticket to witness a master of his craft who (his newspaper write-ups purported) could summon the dead to appear with him on a shabby stage in a tiny, decrepit Boston theater.

Still, even so, standing on the last threshold of the once great profession of theatrical legerdemain, using the one last lie of a thousand lies advanced through three centuries by hundreds of magicians before him, the playhouse was half empty, and a pallor of gloom seemed to hang, foreboding, in the air. His last performance of the season in what was now an abbreviated annual tour of ten cities, and only a scattering of spectators out there, sprinkled with skeptics.

Up here on stage he could feel their hostility and now and then hear their fanged hissing to one another. But at least they didn't laugh. No one had laughed.

Perhaps because Saxon himself seemed so solemn. As though he believed all that he was doing, and they didn't want to spoil it for him. The tiny voices he created from various places out of the darkness. They, of course, knew it was simple to install sound devices and make noises appear from anywhere. Everybody these days knew everything. And the illusion early in the act of goblins and devils. He had reached back over a hundred years to Professor Anderson for that, but the little flash faces emerging from cabinets and boxes were somehow not as mystifying as they once were, and he'd had to rely on his patter, his stage manner, the mild feat of mass audience hypnosis to keep spectators from squirming in their seats. He could cast a mass hypnotic spell on them for a minute or two at a time, no longer, and they were relaxed and interested when they realized what had happened. But that was a trick, too, a psychological sleight-of-hand, not magic.

If the audience felt Joe Saxon was solemn, it wasn't really solemnity so much as a deep, tragic sadness he carried with him everywhere now like a heavy cloak of nostalgia. A nostalgia for a time past when the masters of his craft believed that some day they would become so imbued in the magic to which they were totally devoted that they would eventually, by accident or otherwise, stumble upon dark secrets that would enable them to know and exhibit a true sorcerer's art of supernatural black magic.

Alas, it was never to be. Saxon's stage illusion of death warming to momentary life was closer than anyone had ever come, but it fell short. Like him, it was a fake, and that was the unending source of his sadness. Everything, everywhere was fake. Nothing was real or solid. Dedicate your life to a lie. There is no supernatural. No illusion is a true one. How could it be when the word illusion itself denoted the very emptiness of illusion: that which seems to be, but is not true.

He was over forty, forty-three to be exact, and had no personal illusions left. Half an inch over six feet, with sleek dark hair, and piercing black eyes, there were planes in his face that it seemed to him were becoming more distinct. At what point do you admit they are creases not of just maturity but age? The grand hopes of once were gone. That early first marriage to Helen that had vanished much in the way Mrs. Hermann had each night into the quicksilver of a mirror, after which he himself had almost vanished from the human race, but didn't, because after all there were other women, too many really, none of them the same as the first, none of them love, but functional, female, though he had decided it was that kind of thinking that made a man a cynic, and the dream of once, whatever it had been (he was no longer sure) was blurred: the acid of time dissolving it, washing it away. Yet you go on. Functioning. Making sure never to try to think too clearly.

He was approaching the finale of the act. His own invention, and his masterpiece. At the convention of magicians in Miami last August not one of the other professionals had come close to guessing how it was done, and no less than J. T. Harris, a millionaire amateur they invited each year at the price of picking up the tab for the hall, food, drinks and orchestra, had (whether he would have gone through with it or not) offered a signed blank check if Saxon would reveal details of the secret. He refused, of course. It was probably the last feat of legerdemain in the world that was still a mystery and that gave Saxon a sly edge over his contemporaries. He hinted it wasn't a trick at all but true black magic. They had all smiled, winked at one another, but there were enough devotees who wistfully believed in the origin of magic to harbor in their minds that what Saxon claimed was possible: he had opened a Pandora's box and discovered the source of all dark answers. That made the trick priceless. His last real possession.

Four or five of those professional magicians were out front now, wherever he played there were always a few of them there to marvel at the final illusion, because unlike those who pursue other endeavors in life, a magician is a special breed that in any waking moment seldom thinks of anything but his craft; he is always "on," performing, often unasked, at private parties, "disappearing" highball glasses at dinner in a restaurant, picking a pocket or whatever else in the corridor of some office building and taking fiendish delight in returning a wallet, wrist watch or valuable ring to the startled victim; even asleep the dream was that of conjuring up the unexplained. They were haunted people who inhabited a fantasy world. They came time and again to see Saxon, who was downstage now, at the tip of the perimeter, the lights behind him blacked out. His voice was low, conversational. He seemed humble, suddenly unsure of himself. In the soundless hall, the audience had to strain to hear him.

"I was married once. That was a long time ago. It seems eons ago. Though I have learned since there is no such thing as time or space."

He had rapt attention. The soft words seemed addressed not to an audience but you as an individual, and there was something almost forlorn about Saxon in these closing minutes of the show making it as if you alone knew of his longing and infinite loneliness.

"Those of you who may have read articles about me in one of the news magazines are aware that in the off season from the theater I live an odd and solitary life in an old barn-like apartment on the top floor of a building in San Francisco."

Mingle truth with the illusion.

"It is a barren, solitary existence, but it gives me the solace to meditate . . . and late one night, seated cross-legged in the darkness, holding my mind a blank, playing the worn, old record of a song I had once known in my days with Lida, she slowly appeared before my eyes. I thought I had imagined it, but—"

A gasp from the audience. A soft glow of light was beginning to appear in the darkness behind Saxon. As though unaware of both that and the chilled ripple of excitement out front, he went on:

"—It was Lida. Since then she has appeared many times—"

Behind him, tiny white dots of light shimmered like a miniature replica of the snowflakes outside falling past the flickering gaslight. They gradually began to take the form of a woman.

"I wish I could tell you that she will appear again tonight as she has on so many other evenings. But I can't make that promise. She may have been called to a far beyond. And in any case, Lida is very special. She cannot simply be summoned."

An hysterical female voice from the audience called out, "*She's behind you.*"

Saxon turned, looked upstage, saw the phosphorous of light slowly flesh out. This was the art. The slow, gradual materialization made it authentic. Any magician worth his name could wave a wand and produce Instant Woman out of seeming nothingness. But to do it in graduating steps was a miracle.

"Lida" stood there now: not in the short-skirted garb of the usual magician's assistant. She wore a simple dress, flat-heeled shoes; her tawny blonde hair was pulled back and tied with a green ribbon. She was young, twenty-three, but the audience understood that death knows no age. She had "died" at the age of twenty-three.

There was heavy applause, and when it stopped momentarily, he looked straight at the girl and said, "Thank you, dear."

She glided toward him, and he embraced her, kissing her on the lips.

Profound, shocked silence out front, then the usual, audible whispers of frightened people who couldn't consciously admit to what they were seeing.

"That's not a ghost. It's a live woman."

"Trick. It's a trick."

Louder now, not a whisper: "Fake . . . *fake.*"

As if responding to that callous rudeness, the girl began to dissolve in Saxon's arms.

Hushed, terrifying silence.

The unexpected.

Suddenly she was gone. Vanished. He stood alone on the empty stage, a hurt look on his face. He gazed out at the audience, then very wearily said:

"Good night."

The stage blacked out. Wild applause.

But when the lights came up he, too, was gone.

The applause went on but he did not return for a curtain call. He never did.

Let them think the insulting murmurs of a few that had frightened "Lida" off had cut him so deeply he could not bring himself to come back and bow.

It completed the illusion.

"MAN, *you* are spooky."

She stood at the far end of the dank basement dressing room, plucking the green ribbon off her blonde hair. It fell to her shoulders framing the oval of her pancake made-up face. Once she washed the makeup off it would be a kid face again with big green eyes, freckles around the pug nose, a pout of a mouth. Offstage she wore no makeup at all, not even lipstick which, if you were good-looking enough to get away with it, was the vogue now.

"Hope the audience thought so."

"I'm sure they did. You probably gave them great big goose bumps." Her voice was a soft drawl, and moving up to him now, pulling off false eyelashes, she smiled roguishly. "Of course you give *me* goose bumps every night. But those are a different kind."

Her name was Ellen Hayes and he'd found her in a Chicago discotheque: a topless go-go dancer in a gilded cage that hung from the ceiling. He'd hired her that same night at twice what the club paid her and they rehearsed for two days before opening in that city.

It had been necessary to get a new assistant because the old one, discovering she was pregnant (though not by him) had quit in Cincinnati to fly back to a heartbroken husband she'd abandoned in Dallas. One of life's milestones. Some women didn't know who or what they were until they became pregnant. Then in a sudden, profound realization scene it became very clear.

He generally made it a point to never shack up with whatever pretty assistant shared the stage with him, but Ellen was a pushy, ambitious girl. The word she used to describe herself was *naturalistic*. She had teased him that he was a square, once blurted out "fuddy-duddy," though apologized immediately because deep down she was a compassionate soul, the type who felt so much for other people that she suffered for them. A bleeder is what they call it. Cut your finger and she bleeds.

"I didn't mean to crush you like that. But I'm here, I'm young, I'm healthy, I dig magic like crazy, and I go for you, so why pay for two hotel rooms when we live in one?"

He'd held out in Chicago because she could return home to the apartment she shared with another go-go dancer, but here in Boston they had registered as husband and wife.

Now, in the dressing room, she sat down in front of the mirror and began daubing gobs of cold cream on her face.

"I think it stinks I just get in on the tail end of your tour." Face smeared white, she gazed at him in the mirror. "I could have had a whole new career."

He couldn't define the slight lilt-accent in her voice. French? Southern? A little of both?

"I'm sure you can go back to what you were doing."

"Nobody should have to go back to what they were doing." She turned on the chair, the green eyes looking as though they were shiny jewels in the snow. "Will you take me back to San Francisco with you?"

He shook his head. "I live a very monastic life during the off season."

"Does that mean no broads?"

"Unless I invite them in. You see, I prefer to live alone."

"Boy, I must be a real lousy lay."

"You're a great lay."

She picked up a towel and began rubbing off the cold cream. The steam-heated room was very hot. He took off his coat and sat down beside her in front of the big mirror.

There was an odd, wounded look in her eyes, then she glanced over and said brightly: "All right, I'll level with you. What I really want to do is go to Las Vegas. I don't have the fare. But if I got as far as San Francisco—"

"You little bitch."

She nodded, unashamed. "I was going to leave you high and dry as soon as we arrived and take a Greyhound bus from there."

Had that been her plan? Or was it a cover-up because she had offered herself and had been rejected?

"Bet I could do real great in Las Vegas."

"They don't pay the showgirls too much."

"But it'd be a start," she said. "I could be seen. People from Hollywood, California, go to Las Vegas. Whoever goes to any place in Chicago? Man, what a dump, creep town that is."

He was about to give his own evaluation of Chicago when there was a rap on the door, muffled voices outside, one of them a woman.

"I *must* see him."

Ellen was on her feet, looking for a place to hide. He had instructed her that "Lida" could never be seen by anyone who had been to the performance. The illusion of her unearthly appearance had to be maintained. She couldn't be found in a dressing room removing makeup.

On the other side of the door, a man was saying, "Madam, I've told you, he doesn't see anybody."

The door burst open and a small, plump, hysterical woman barged in, her shabby cloth coat wet with shreds of icy snow. The stage door guard stood out in the corridor behind her, harassed. Ellen threw the cold cream towel over her face and turned away. She looked ludicrous. Saxon got to his feet, trying both to distract the woman and to block her view of Ellen.

"Lady, he's right, I never receive visitors."

He paused then, for she was looking up at him in awe, her mouth open as though she found herself in the presence of deity. She was dowdy, in her forties. It's funny, he thought, how I always notice a woman is in her forties but never remember I myself am that age. We who are us, singularly us, have no age. We are only ourselves. It is the others who change, age, wilt. Even our mirror lies. We are the same golden person forever. Oh, God, the self-deception we perpetrate on our craven souls. All right, she's in her forties, look more closely, see her as she looked before, the way she still sees herself: a golden person, a broken human being with a candle of hope somehow lighting a way to go on. Yes, she was pretty. She *is* pretty. Laughter had forsaken her as if forever. But she is pretty. Soft, humble.

"It's all right, Ed," he told the stage door guard, "I'll talk to her."

Ed nodded and moved away. It was drafty now, but Saxon left the dressing room door open in the hope the woman wouldn't stay more than a few moments. Ellen still wore the cold cream towel over her head. She looked so damned stupid he couldn't stand it.

"You," he said, "unmask."

Ellen took off the towel, and the woman, staring past Saxon, saw her. She gasped, huddling back against the cold, gray perspiring wall.

"She's here with you."

"Lady, what is it you want?"

"She went away up there on stage. She vanished. But I knew she'd come back to you."

Ellen saw the agony on the woman's face and was compelled by it. Nobody got to anybody the way everybody got to Ellen.

Saxon, concentrating on the woman, said: "If you'll just compose yourself—"

She turned back to him now.

"It's about my husband. You're the only one who can help me."

He knew what was coming, and it was this kind of thing he most wanted to avoid.

"We were very close," the woman was saying, "he was all I had. But a year ago he was killed. In a car accident. I was with him, but I wasn't even badly hurt. I feel so guilty about it."

"You mustn't."

"I have to reach him. I must get through. I know he's still here. Earthbound. He's at home with me. In fact, he's in here now. This very minute. I feel it, I know it."

She was crying.

"But I can't talk to him. It's just silence. I can't communicate. I've been to mediums. They say they can help, but they don't, they can't. They're cheats. All of them. Liars. But you can bring him to me. Even if it's only for a precious minute. I'll pay you. I don't have a lot of money, but I'll pay you."

He felt the awful enormity of her problem and realized the only poor gift he could offer was truth.

"Madam, I can't help you. I can scarcely help myself."

The woman looked stricken. She pointed at Ellen. "But—you—"

"That isn't Lida," Saxon said. "Ellen is a go-go dancer from Chicago. There isn't any Lida. It's a name I made up for my act. I do have an ex-wife but her name is Helen and she's still alive."

"I don't believe you."

"There is no supernatural, no such thing as a ghost," Saxon told her. "I've spent my life looking for evidence in the here-after, but it isn't there. The dead are dead and forever dead."

"No . . ."

He despised the role of a Dear Abby but she had come to him for comfort and he owed it to his conscience to be honest.

"There is no spirit world. The bereft are condemned to go on alone. Make yourself realize that. It's the only chance you have for happiness. Instead of looking back, plan a new life."

But the lady in her forties would not, could not believe him, and seeing Ellen's sudden gentle tears, turned to her.

"You *are* Lida, aren't you?"

"Yes."

Saxon stared at Ellen, hearing the woman in the wet cloth coat saying to him:

"You lied to me."

"But there's something you must understand," Ellen went on. "He can't summon me, let alone any of the others who are out there, such as your husband. That's why he told you what he did."

Ellen approached and Saxon saw the woman tremble at being in such close proximity to a wraith. Yet, even so, she was absorbing and believing every word.

"I came to him of my own free will," Ellen said. "That's the way it has to be with you and your husband. Go home and concentrate and maybe he will appear. Perhaps for just that one precious minute you asked for."

Saxon suppressed a desire to strangle Ellen.

"And later if you think you only imagined you saw him it doesn't matter, because that's the way it happens sometimes. You see a loved one in your mind. But it's just as real as I am standing here in front of you."

Staring at Ellen, the woman had grown visibly pale with the nameless terror only the dead can evoke.

"Thank you," she murmured gratefully, "thank you."

She turned and hurried out.

Saxon closed the dressing room door, glaring at Ellen who began retreating.

"What the hell kind of crap was that?"

Ellen was a marvelous, talented liar. Proof of that was the way she had conned the woman, and now, moving back and forth between mirror and wall she was prepared for Saxon's onslaught. Instead of frankly admitting she had pitied the woman and didn't want her to be let down, she shouted:

"Maybe *you* want to give away the secret of your great stage illusion free of charge, but I just couldn't let you. Do you want some poor, baggy-assed widow loud-mouthing it all over Boston that your act is a fake? That 'Lida' is a go-go dancer, for Christ's sake?"

He couldn't believe what he was hearing.

"All right, I realize you felt sorry for her." She had lowered her voice. "But that's no excuse. I *had* to go on being Lida to protect you from yourself." She wiped at tears. "And by the way, you never did tell me whether you're going to let me go as far as San Francisco with you. I mean, after all, two in a compartment on those trains can't cost much more than it would for one."

He sighed gently. "All right, Ellen, you're aboard."

She sat down with her back to the mirror and looked up at him.

"I'll be great in Las Vegas once I get my break. Betcha I make a hit." She swung around facing the mirror, but watching him in the glass as if trying to read his face. "You believe that, don't you? That I'll make it big there?"

WOODEN WHEELS clattering over the ruts and pits out there on that dark, flat prairie; he didn't know how the hell people managed to survive those long treks in broken-down covered wagons. And now this monster of steel, car after car of it, hurtling through the night, the lights from its windows spilling past the stark silhouette of barren trees and tumbleweed and gopher holes and rock and railside shacks and red, flashing wig-wag signals that clanged for only an instant in the rush of speed, the sound then swallowed whole into silence; the sway of the cars, the staccato click of railroad ties, this, too, was an outmoded means of transportation across the apron of America, its towns, villages, plowed fields, farms, mountains, rivers, dark woods, its tranquil eternity, but Saxon had two trunks filled with props, more luggage than a streaking jet airliner would permit, and he always traveled with the accoutrements of his magic.

"You're not paying attention," Ellen said.

They'd had the porter bring a card table into the compartment, and she was sitting across from him clad in a green turtleneck sweater that matched her eyes, yellow hair piled up on her head, her face scrubbed, not a trace of makeup. He wondered if he could count the freckles around her nose.

"No, look at the cards, not at me."

She held up a deck of cards face out.

"Go ahead, pick a card, any card. But don't let me see it." That vague accent again, lilting, pretty.

He smiled wanly. She realized she was in way over her head exhibiting sleight-of-hand before a professional magician, but it seemed to amuse her to try. He slipped a card from the deck, careful not to let her see it was the three of hearts, and handed it back. She buried it with the other cards and pushed them over to him.

"Now shuffle."

He riffled the cards, shuffling them well, tempted to make each individual card dance across the top of his fingers the way he once had in the old days, but this was her act and he wouldn't cramp it. He handed her the deck.

Looking at the backs of the playing cards she rapidly cast them down one by one, and then, in small triumph, turned up the three of hearts.

"Is that it?"

"Yes, that's the card. Amazing."

"Do you know how I did it?"

"Before returning it to the deck you creased the lower right hand corner with your fingernail."

She pouted. "Spoil sport." Then: "Would you like me to do another even more amazing trick?"

"By all means. Proceed."

She held up the fingernail-creased three of hearts, closed her hand over it, then opening her hand, it was gone. He knew it was wedged between the fingers on the side of the hand he could not see but it had been a very adroit move, close to professional, and he was damned if he was going to be a spoil sport again.

"That's terrific."

This time she didn't risk asking whether he knew how she had done it.

"I studied magic once."

With a snap of her finger the three of hearts magically reappeared and she returned it to the deck. They'd had dinner brought in earlier tonight. The tray of dishes was still here and she reached back to it, picked up the salt shaker and a cloth napkin.

"Got a dime?"

He fished into his pocket, got out a dime and handed it to her.

"This feat of magic will really rock you," she said. "I'm going to make that dime go right through the table."

Clang, clang, clang. Lights of rural houses flashing past the dark window.

She placed the dime under the salt shaker, folded the napkin over it, and watching him, her face impish, began shaping the napkin over it. Then she banged her hand down, lifted up the napkin-enclosed salt shaker, held it over her lap. The dime was still there on the table. Seeming vexed, she wet her finger and rubbed it on the bottom of the salt shaker. This was a feint to make the spectator suspect she would cause the dime to stick there. She set the salt shaker down, banging on it again, again lifting it, wrapped in the napkin. But the pesky dime was still in place. Frowning, she once more put the napkin on the table and hit it with her fist. This time the napkin flattened under the impact and when she lifted it the dime was still there but, lo and behold, the salt shaker was gone.

"Marvelous," he said.

"Don't I make a good magician's assistant?"

"Yes, you're—in fact, *you're* spooky."

She had covertly let the salt shaker slip from the napkin into her lap; the cloth had retained its mold when she put it back on the table, and while the audience was presumably still concentrating on the dime, she pulled the switch.

She reached down now, as if to the floor, and came up with the salt shaker. She put it back on the table, then sat back, gazing at him.

"Four months on the road with your show. That makes your off season eight whole months. What do you do during all that time?"

He gave her an odd look. "I thought you knew."

"In the two and a half weeks we've been together you haven't told me boo about yourself."

"There's been publicity. I assumed it was general knowledge."

"Who has time to read? Clue me in."

"I have another profession."

Her face fell. "I thought you were a full-fledged magician."

"I am."

"A really dedicated magician wouldn't dream of doing anything else."

He smiled. "These days he has to. Like the circus, acts of pure magic are fading away."

"They still have the circus. I see it on TV."

"Unfortunately, so does almost everybody else."

"All right, what's your other profession?"

"It relates to magic, if that makes you feel any better. You really *do* dig magic, don't you?"

She nodded. "Ever since I was knee high to a grasshopper."

"It's because I have a reputation of knowing every facet

and device ever invented to mystify man I got the first assign-ment. Somebody who felt I would have the answers wanted his place *un*mystified."

"Maybe I'm dense, but I don't—"

"I'm a psychic detective." She looked startled, and he went on: "Not that I think that's an apt description of what I do. In fact, it's an exaggeration. Let's just say, to put it crudely, I'm a ghost-breaker."

She was staring at him. "You make money at it?"

"From time to time."

"Exactly what is it you do?"

"My first job was a house out in the desert a few miles from Palm Springs, an expensive property, walled in, with a swim-ming pool and cactus garden, but it had been empty for more than a year. The owner was in Europe and hadn't been able to rent it. During his absence, what with wind storms, rain and vandals, it was in pretty bad shape. Then a rumor spread that it was haunted."

"It sounds haunted," she said. She got up, and swaying with the movement of the train, cleaned off the card table. "Why would anybody want to build a house all by itself way out there on a lonely stretch of desert?"

"Some people like seclusion."

She folded the table and placed it beside the compartment door, then curled up on the seat, looking at him like a child ready to be spooked out of her mind by a ghost story.

"Go on."

"During Easter vacation a couple of teen-agers slipped in, intending to stay until morning. However, certain ghostly oc-currences drove them out before midnight. They returned at one A.M. with reinforcements—four or five of their buddies, very tough, skeptical kids who didn't think anything on earth could frighten them. They fled within an hour."

Her eyes were large. "*What was happening in that house?*"

"I'll come to that. The house was on the market to be sold for an asking price of forty-five thousand—even though it had cost considerably more to build. But nobody was interested and the real estate broker who had the listing wrote to the owner and told him why: the place was spooked. He advised him to cut the price to half or less, though, adding he doubted he could even sell it at that figure. The owner wasn't able to come back from Europe but cabled an outside appraiser to inspect the house and suggest a selling price. The appraiser simply could not believe that that or any other property was haunted. He decided to spend the night there."

"Did *he* get spooked?"

"I never met the man but I'm told before morning he was running all over that house in near hysterics. He was taken to the hospital with a nervous breakdown."

"God," she said.

"In desperation, the owner contacted me long-distance from Paris. Somebody had told him about the unearthly hallucinations I had created on stage. He didn't believe in ghosts, and when I told him I didn't either, he put me on the case."

"He felt anybody who could create an unearthly hallucination should be able to expose one."

"Right," Saxon said. "I went to Palm Springs posing as another outside real estate appraiser. I announced that I, too, would spend the night in that house."

She scrooched back on the seat, put her legs up, clasped her arms around her knees and waited for him to relate what he had experienced.

It was a deathly quiet night, not a breath of wind, and as he drove along the narrow, rutted road the scenic desert landscape bathed in red-yellow hues of a full moon looked as though it had been painted there. He saw the two-story, walled-in house in the distance, dark, solitary, a cascade of stars glittering high above, seeming in this awesome cone of silence like a beckoning infinite.

He stopped his car before the rusted iron gates, got out, pressed a key into the padlock, and when it sprung free, pushed the gates open. On previous visits to the place vandals had scaled the wall. He drove in, parked, noticing when he cut the car's motor that the enveloping silence was even more intense. It seemed unbelievable any place in a world of the living could be so devoid of sound.

The house stood before him, bleak, foreboding, its sand-brown edifice peeling; he heard the scrunch of his shoes on gravel as he moved to the massive front door. He had brought along a flashlight and two candles complete with holders, but not any ghost-breaking equipment, if indeed any such thing existed. He relied solely on his knowledge of seemingly unexplainable sorcery and utter, disdaining disbelief of anything whatsoever that could be attributed to the supernatural.

Inside the house, he beamed the flashlight around the huge living room, seeing rafters in the ceiling, the hardwood floor, a giant fireplace, curtainless windows scudded with skeins of sand, but nothing whatsoever unusual. It was simply an empty house.

He lit the candles, placing one on the mantel above the fireplace, and the other on the floor at the far side of the room. They sputtered, then casting grotesque shadows, flickered brightly, providing enough light for him to keep a constant survey. He walked about then, from dining room to kitchen, and out on a porch-den that through French doors faced the empty, sand-damaged swimming pool in the back yard.

Except for the echo of his footsteps on the hardwood floor, all was a tomb of silence.

He had returned to the living room and started for the stairs to the second floor when he thought he heard something, though it had been so indistinct he could not be sure. He stood motionless, listening, then heard it again and this time was positive.

Hoarse, whispery coughing.

He directed the beam of his flashlight to the fireplace. There was no one visible. He stared through the candlelit room and saw nothing.

The coughing grew noisier, an agonized, hacking cough.

Though he had prepared himself to be ready for anything, it seemed to him here in this empty house hackles were rising on the back of his neck.

The coughing stopped, there was a moan, a choking, distraught moan as though made by a man whose throat is cut. Saxon was drawn toward the fireplace. He was not yet there when his nostrils were assaulted by a whiff of rotting, stagnant odor, and then footsteps could be heard as an unseen thing seemed to brush by him, the stench in the air now nauseating. The word death leapt to his mind. The smell of death. He turned, peering through the murky gloom at nothing and heard the footsteps mounting the stairs.

Saxon no longer tried to reason. Galvanized into action, he raced to the stairs and took them two at a time in pursuit of the unseen. Reaching the second floor, he beamed the flashlight one way, then the other. The sound of footsteps had stopped but a door at the end of the airless corridor slammed shut.

He walked up to the door, took a deep breath, then opened it and walked into a dusty, barren bedroom, its bare floor glowing like blood in the reddish moonlight filtering through the window. Saxon stood there, looking around. Nothing, nobody. Skeptic though he was, he felt an icy tingle crawl up his spine like clammy skeleton fingers.

Now a creaking noise, and as he watched, a closet door slowly swung open, a strangling odor of decomposed flesh reeking from the inky darkness within. No matter how much one disbelieved, it was unnerving and, trembling, licking his dry mouth, he raised the flashlight and cast its white glow into the empty closet. Nothing.

Driven from the room by the odor, Saxon returned up the hall to the stairs and started down. When he reached the sanctuary of the candlelit living room he breathed a little easier, then froze. A formless white shape was standing in front of the fireplace.

The train whistle shrieked, howling wind carrying it back across the top of the speeding metal cars in a savage whine. Not immediately identifying the sound and already terrified by what Saxon was describing, Ellen screamed.

It shook him up. "What's the matter with you?"

"I'm sorry." She was still too nervous to smile. "I don't know which scared me worse—you or that train whistle. All right now, you were saying—that ghost was there."

"I didn't say it was a ghost."

"Never mind. What did you do?"

"Stayed there in the house and waited."

"You've got guts, I'll admit that."

"Nothing else happened. The odor evaporated and the white substance vanished. Then, two hours later, the whole performance was repeated. That was when I realized a timing device was involved. By daylight I had found the gimmicks and ingredients used to create sound, a terrible odor, and a puff of phosphorous smoke. Even the opening and closing of doors was triggered by a simple electronic bug."

She pouted. "You've just ruined the whole thing."

26

"The materials required for that kind of set-up can only be bought at certain places. I traced it back and uncovered the culprit."

"Who was it?"

"The real estate man who had the listing on the house. A couple from the East had been out two years before and wanted the place. They, of course, had heard nothing about it being haunted and felt it would be a steal at thirty-seven thousand."

"So the broker wanted to beat down the owner's price."

Saxon nodded. "Buy it himself for eighteen or twenty thousand, spend another two to have it restored."

"And then resell it to the couple from the East. But what if somebody told them it was haunted?"

"It *wouldn't* be any more and they could laugh off such superstitious rumors as nonsense."

"People," Ellen said disgustedly.

"That's right. Everything's a hoax."

"You've exposed others."

"All over the world. The story of the house in the desert was published in a magazine and after that I was besieged by people who up to then had been convinced they were being financially done in by ghosts. Most of it is in Europe. England. Ireland. There are more 'ghosts' per capita in Ireland than anywhere else on earth. Unless it's Germany."

For several moments now the train rattled on the tracks, the car they were in swaying almost violently, then the roll stopped, all was smooth again, emphasizing the steady *click click click* of the ties scuttling by underneath.

She had been gazing at him. "You mean it? You don't believe in the supernatural?"

"Not a whit. And even if I had, the business I'm in would have disillusioned me beyond all hope of ever believing anything."

"There's never been any real proof of a ghost?"

"Not even any unreal proof."

It seemed incredible to her. "Absolutely *nothing* that hasn't been logically explained?"

Seated by the window, his face was pensive, brooding, and there was again that almost forlorn look in the black, probing eyes that theater audiences now and then detected.

"It's not that I haven't wanted to believe," he said. "The unknown is the very source of true magic. But it isn't there. There is no truth."

"Everything is a hoax."

"I'm afraid so. Though," he added, "there *are* one or two mysteries left. Poltergeists, for instance. They have a scientific explanation, but it can't be proven."

"What the hell's a poltergeist?"

He rose, stretched. "Let's go up to the club car and have a drink."

"Fine with me."

She, too, got up.

Before they left the compartment he opened a suitcase, palmed a small object, and with the dexterity of the great magician he was, vanished it into a secret lining inside his jacket.

❧IV❧

ELLEN never wore a bra, and now here in the club car the train was jiggling again and so were her straight-out breasts beneath the fabric of the green turtleneck sweater. It reminded him of the first time he had seen those beautiful teats joggling up and down there in that gilded cage hanging above a trio of manic musicians; but he hadn't lusted for her then, nor did he now, particularly; it was as simple as: it is pleasant, even warm in her company. A three-day train trip across the continent can become monotonous and he was delighted she had prevailed upon him to let her come along.

"All right," she said, "what is a poltergeist?"

He didn't answer at once. The car seemed small, intimate, or at least this section of it: a five-seater bar with a large mirror, shelves of glasses and a row of copper Moscow Mule cups, a band of metal acting as a guard rail so they wouldn't fall off. There were several tables. He and Ellen were at one of them, two other couples seated across the way. They were older, in their fifties, both women (at least in his eyes) quite attractive. One of them after staring at Saxon turned and whispered into her husband's ear. The man looked over, his eyes brightening. He nodded to his wife, smiled "hello" to Saxon. Saxon smiled back. They had recognized him. It is older people, he thought, with yesterday's memories, who still travel on trains, and still remember the heyday of The Great Saxon.

A pair of hard-headed businessmen were plunked down at the bar, one bald-headed and glassy-eyed, continually saying he had to go back to his room, the other with silver grey hair and a trim silver grey moustache who continually insisted he had one more racy joke to tell.

"A poltergeist is presumably a child ghost that plays pranks."

"How can a *child* ghost go unexplained by science and not an adult ghost?"

"Because the explanation precludes the word 'ghost.' But that's a good question."

"Wow," Ellen said. "From now on I'm going to be full of questions."

He looked up and saw rain slapping against the dark windows: the train rushing through a storm; lightning flashed, the turbulent night sky revealing a jagged streak of white that seemed to point at them like a finger, but the clap of thunder that must have accomplished it was lost in the grind of iron wheels on a steel track.

"A poltergeist," he said, "causes things like dishes and such to fly through the air. There have been many incidents where experts were present and couldn't explain it. In one celebrated case in Long Island, police, reporters and even a TV camera were on hand, yet dishes, lamps, ashtrays still flew about wildly. No gimmicks, no answer. Except—"

There he stopped.

"Except?"

Her breasts were no longer jiggling, instead now quivered

with the movement of the train and he was suddenly aware he was looking forward to being alone with her tonight. It startled him. The contrary nature of man. It meant he *was* lusting when only a moment before he had assumed he wasn't. He wondered exactly when the lust had begun. Now? At this particular moment? And why? He had been with her several nights. Why was it now different? What, after all, is the answer to man except another baffling unknown?

"Except? God, go on."

"I think we need another drink."

He signalled the colored bar porter, who started mixing fresh drinks.

"Except whenever a poltergeist has performed," Saxon said, "a young child has been present. And, by the way, there have been hundreds of verified poltergeist reports. One took place in a small, rural schoolhouse in Wisconsin. They had a pot-bellied stove in the room with a bucket of coal beside it. All at once chunks of coal flew up out of the bucket and began pelting the teacher and the students. They hid under desks, lay on the floor, terrified, and finally the bucket itself began to rise and for a full minute or two hung suspended in space."

Ellen shivered. The couples across the car had eavesdropped, and were still, interested. At last Ellen said:

"But what can a child have to do with—"

"—Childish pranks? Scientists and even psychiatrists have offered a theory that a repressed or disturbed child has within him a dynamo of resentment so great he can order a hurtling chaos of inanimate objects out of sheer will power."

"God Almighty," Ellen said, "that in itself is spooky."

"Yes, I admit it is."

"How can you say that if a living child can will unanswerable feats, a repressed or disturbed dead person can't?"

"Because that phenomenon has never been proven."

"Have you been *everywhere?* At all places throughout history where ghosts have been reported?"

"No, of course not."

The other two couples kept listening raptly, but Saxon did not look at them.

"Then what do you really know except what you've learned in your own limited experience with frauds?"

"Nothing. You're right about that."

He looked sharply in the direction of the bar, and she followed his gaze. One of the Moscow Mule cups lifted from behind the protective metal strip. It rose slowly, hung in mid-air. Everybody saw it except the porter, who was on his way over with the drinks Saxon had ordered, and the bald-headed man seated bleary-eyed on a stool still whining that he should go to his room.

"Look," one of the women gasped.

The porter had put the drinks down now, and turned in time to see the suspended cup suddenly whiz past the bald-headed man's ear. As it crashed to the floor, he stumbled to his feet, weaving.

"Who threw that? *You?*"

Then the bald-headed man realized he was staring at himself in the bar mirror, had addressed the question to his own reflection, and obviously deciding he was too drunk to press the probe further, turned and lurched to the door. The man with the trim, silver grey moustache swung around on his stool. He was ashen. The two couples across the car from Saxon sat tensely, unable to comprehend what they had seen. Ellen, too, was spellbound. The porter picked up the cup, ready to attribute what had happened to some queer jerk of the train.

But now a second copper cup slipped its mooring, rose up, drifted to the middle of the car and hung there a-tremble for a moment before falling. Ellen shot Saxon a quick look.

"*You're* making that happen."

The four people across the car seemed relieved, smiled, gazed at him, and in deep admiration, applauded. The porter and the man with the grey moustache gawked at Saxon.

One of the women said, "He's the world's most celebrated magician."

The porter let out his breath, gently mopped at perspiration, and looking at Saxon, said ruefully: "Man, that was downright scary."

He returned behind the bar.

Ellen was watching Saxon closely now, but he had palmed the small electro-magnetic ray so adroitly she had been completely unaware when he secreted it back in the lining of his jacket.

"What do you mean *I* made it happen?" he said innocently, as though wounded. "Had to be a poltergeist."

"There aren't any children present."

He smiled. "Destroys the whole poltergeist theory, doesn't it?"

"You said those kind of things can't be done with gimmicks."

"They can't. Not with the force and vitality a real poltergeist demonstrates."

"Then it *was* a trick?"

"I'm not saying."

One of the men across the way asked: "How are you able to make the object go at different speeds, and then, finally, just hang there?"

"I ask it to."

The people laughed.

On the way back through the swaying cars, he explained to Ellen: "I invented that gadget trying to duplicate the antics of a true poltergeist, but it's only partially successful."

In the compartment, she closed and locked the door, then turned.

"I'm not going to like having to say goodbye to you in San Francisco."

He was seated on the bed slipping off his shoes. "Kid, tell you something, I'll miss you, too."

"Since when did I become 'kid'?"

"Time I reminded myself."

"Why *now?*"

He frowned, looking up at her. "Wasn't going to tell you, but maybe it's best I do. I have a friend in San Francisco."

The shade was still up and rain was streaking along the window.

"A girl friend?"

He nodded. "Been with her a long time. Good many years. She's come to depend on me. Maybe the truth is, it's also the other way around."

"Well, I guess there's nothing like a good vintage wine."

She flipped off her sweater and here in the dim light he saw her naked breasts. He reached over and pulled down the window shade.

"Ellen, if I were younger, and starting out again, it'd be you."

"Thanks." She was hurt. Now she added: "You're young enough. Don't you think you are?"

He tried to explain it to her. "As the years go by you come to realize there are certain things you owe to people."

Unzipping her skirt, she stepped out of it, clad now only in sheer black scanty-panties; then undid her hair and tilted her head, looking down at him, blonde hair dipping past one side of her face, the other half in shadow.

"Why doesn't she go on tour with you?"

"Has a child to raise."

He tried not to look at her, tried instead to concentrate on Marge. Red-headed Marge. Thank God she wouldn't be at the station to meet him. He hadn't sent the usual telegram saying when he expected to arrive so she had no way of knowing.

"Your child?"

"No," he said. "She's a divorcee."

"Why don't you marry her?"

"Because I'm not home very much, and besides, I'm not a family man. It wouldn't be good for me, or fair to them. Probably, if you analyze it, what I am is a cold-blooded bastard of some kind, because it's true I spend most of my time alone. And laugh if you want, I *do* meditate. I'm what you might call a classic introvert."

"Excuses," Ellen said. "Men always have excuses. If you loved her you'd marry her."

"I don't know. You may be right."

She sat down beside him on the bed. "What it really adds up to is you don't want to hurt her."

He looked straight ahead. "Or anybody. Not if I can help it. But especially her."

"Well," she said, "it's been a nice train trip."

Later, in bed, clinging to him, she was out of breath, but even so, bitter.

"This is magic too, isn't it?"

"No. Almost every man has this kind of magic."

Whispering now: "I don't believe that. It's not possib——"

The whisper trailed out into a soft moan.

IT WAS A DARK, dreamless sleep, his mind a void, and he lay very still, breathing almost imperceptibly, the way it had been a few years ago when he was laid out in a coffin six feet under the ground, hands clasped across his chest, holding himself in a trance-like, cataleptic state so as not to consume more than the measured cubic feet of air in the closed, black box before his assistant ordered it dug up and carted to the theater in time for Saxon to emerge and begin the matinee performance. That had been in the summer when they moved from town to town doing one-day stands, and it was good ballyhoo to announce in advance The Great Saxon would be buried alive in the local cemetery; there was always a crowd on hand to see the casket lowered into the grave, those same people later paying admission to witness his "rise from the dead" before commencing other acts. It was an excellent come-on, all right, but also was once almost the end of him, that day in Charden, Ohio, when it was raining, and the heavy wet earth caved in the lid of the flimsy coffin. He reached for the cord that would ring a small bell above ground signalling he was in trouble, but it was stuck fast in mud. He tugged and pulled to no avail, rivulets of water, dirt and slime pouring over him, then he remembered too late he depended on one portion of precious air to filter into the coffin through loose, dry earth. He had thought: this is a terrible way to die. And what he felt was black dread. Horror. The telegraph of his mind shot out frantic bolts of panic, muted cries for help. He pulled again and again on the cord, but it was immovable; then, beginning to suffocate, he heard a clatter of spades overhead. Later, on the surface, his face and clothing dripping mud, his assistant explained he had experienced a sudden, urgent premonition.

Saxon told him the "premonition" was actually ESP. "I got through to you." But his employee didn't believe in extra sensory perception and was damned if he was going to credit Saxon with saving his own life.

Now, here on the train, Saxon's subconscious began to flash *Wake up*, feebly at first, but at last with jolting clarity, *Wake up*. He stirred, opened his eyes, then saw Ellen sitting on the edge of the bed, fully clothed in a short blue skirt and a yellow blouse. When she saw he was awake she became ecstatic.

"I did it. I did it."

He propped himself up on one elbow. "You did what?"

She stuck a cigarette between his lips and lit it for him. "Woke you up with my silent alarm clock. The one inside my head."

"Baby, would you raise the shade?"

"Sure."

She put up the blind. The train was streaking across a soggy green valley still wet with yesterday's rain; the sky was black, ominous.

"You can wake anybody up by just sitting and staring at them."

"Yes, but what wakes them up? What woke *you* up? I was

concentrating." He just looked at her, and she went on, irritated: "Here, look, it's an hour earlier than you usually come to." She picked up his wrist watch and showed it to him. "I was very quiet, didn't jar the bed or anything. I just stared at you. It was ESP."

He sat up, putting his feet on the floor. "What do you know about ESP?"

"I know it exists. I've read about it, and I've heard of it all my life. For instance, there's a story my grandmother tells. There was this little village in Europe somewhere. A woman's husband was struck by lightning. The funeral was the next day, but a few hours later she got obsessed by some idea he was trying to reach her. Her relatives did their best to calm her down and that night finally persuaded her to go to bed. But she couldn't sleep. She screamed that her husband was calling for her. The relatives took her to a doctor. Even a sedative didn't help. By morning she was such a sobbing wreck they agreed to dig up the grave, and when they opened the coffin they saw the man lying there, dead, his eyes wide open in terror, his hair torn out, clutched between his fingers, and the satin lining of the coffin clawed to shreds. He had been buried alive and *had* been trying to reach his wife for help." Standing there, she paused, swaying with the movement of the car, and looked down at him. "Well? Can you believe that?"

He hesitated before answering because there was a sudden chill settling over him. "Yes, I believe it."

"You *do?* You actually do?"

He pinched out the cigarette. "Why shouldn't I?"

Clang, clang, clang.

Railroad crossing. Wig-wag signal. Houses in a small town rocketing by. People out there gazing at the train. A child waving. Then the town was gone. Farmland, a highway in the distance, automobiles traveling along it.

"Because you claim to be such a skeptic. And isn't ESP a mystery of life? Like poltergeists?"

"Some people might say that. However, I believe it's generally accepted. There are departments in several big universities devoted to the study of ESP. Among other things, they've verified reports that women on the very day a son was killed in a war many thousands of miles away were electrified at hearing his voice cry out to them. In most cases, audibly." He paused. "How come you woke me up so early?"

"Because we'll be in San Francisco by noon. That means my last few hours with you are running out."

Her green eyes looked as if they might cry.

"Pity," he said, "it really is."

Eagerly now: "In the time that's left could we practice ESP?"

"Are you sure I need practice?"

"*I* do. The subject fascinates me. And I've worked it all out. While you're shaving I'll go to the dining car. I'll put the food chit you write the order on in front of me, hold a pencil poised, and make my mind a blank. Meanwhile, you concentrate hard on what you want for breakfast. Keep repeating it mentally. When I think I have the message I'll jot it down, and here in the compartment, you do the same thing, write it out, then when you come in we'll compare notes."

When he slid open the dining car door he saw her a few tables away, seated by the window, frowning down at the food order, and now it was he who thought: the hours with you are running out. It struck him as odd he should feel that slight, aching pang for someone he knew so little about, had been with such a brief time, and would never see again. But he had learned better than to try and make a casual encounter part of his life. It was always a spark that soon died, and the longer you lingered, hanging on, the worse the hurt when it ended.

Her brows furrowed, she did not look up as he approached, and he noticed the slim vase on the table with a single rose in it, and the dark, wooded landscape gliding by outside. Now she saw him.

"Oh," a little startled, "I didn't expect you quite so soon."

He sat down on the other side of the table. "Write the order?"

She nodded, pushing the food chit to him, and he placed his list beside it. The items were identical, even in the same order:

> Orange juice
> Oatmeal
> Poached eggs
> Coffee

"They're exactly alike," she said excitedly, then: "See? See?"

"Ellen, I hate to, but there's something I have to point out. I've ordered the same thing the past two mornings."

She slumped, gazed out the window, then looked back. "That was a dirty trick. Why didn't you change it?"

"Didn't occur to me. I just wrote what came to mind."

"Then it's possible we *were* on the same wave length."

"Could be."

She meditated a moment, then shrugged. "Oh, well, maybe ESP is only meant to be used in times of crisis." She gazed at him, her face wistfully tender. "Anyway, it's been wonderful knowing you, Joe."

"I feel the same way about you."

Outside the window, rain began to fall again. It came down in a torrent.

He didn't trust himself to ask her to stay over for a day or two, and after the train was safely docked at the station they went by cab to the Greyhound terminal. It was still pouring rain and she was now wearing a matching set: glistening white raincoat, hat and galoshes. He waited in the bus depot while she was at the window buying a one-way ticket out of his life. She returned, carrying the ticket, her scrubbed face looking innocent and young under the shiny white rain hat.

"The Las Vegas bus doesn't leave until five. But don't you worry. I'll buy a magazine to read and wait here."

"I wouldn't think of it," he said. "We'll have lunch somewhere—at Fisherman's Wharf, matter of fact. I may as well show you the tourist sights. Then we'll run up to my place and you can have a look at it. It's a real curiosity."

"I'd *love* to see where you live. Can't we have lunch there? Catered by a delicatessen or something?"

"I suppose so. That is, if you can stand liverwurst sandwiches."

"Anything, Joe."

It was a loft on the top floor of a battered office building that had been erected after the 1906 earthquake, its big, scenic front window overlooked almost all of San Francisco, and once you were inside there was a certain warmth, a feeling of grandeur, what with the rococo decor, a thick, wine-red Chinese rug wall to wall, and large, sturdy pieces of antique furniture.

"I live in a past age," Saxon explained.

There was a massive old table, fit for a palace banquet, a large, old-fashioned bed, a tremendous stone fireplace, and priceless smaller pieces, divans, love-seats, stools, chairs scattered over the ninety-foot room. Across that wide expanse from the scenic window where a gray tarnish of rain now poured down outside, stood the opposite wall totally covered by a faded, red velvet theater curtain.

"That was the curtain in the first theater that permitted me to present my magic," Saxon said. "When I heard they were going to tear the place down I cabled and asked if I could buy it."

"Cabled?"

"The Mercury Theatre in Plymouth, England. I had to go abroad for my first chance. And now that curtain is old, fading, and so am I."

"You're not!" she said. "God damn it, you're not!"

"I feel it sometimes."

"I think you brood too much."

He nodded. "Always looking in dark places for something that isn't there." Then he brightened. "Some entertainers keep scrapbooks full of clippings. I don't. I have my own way of preserving the past."

He stepped to the side of the wall, pressed a button and the velvet curtain parted, opening just as it once had in the Mercury Theatre in Plymouth, England, so long ago; and a tube of neon lighting flickered on from below much like footlights. Ellen's eyes widened. The entire wall was a multicolored mural reproducing an exact replica of old theatrical posters that not only advertised "Saxon The Great," but depicted him either bound by chains or ropes, or beside an illusion he had performed on stage: a bloody decapitated head on a tray; a very much alive half-lady seen from the torso up; a veiled princess floating in space; a coffin being lowered into a grave combined with a picture of the same coffin on stage, Saxon climbing out of it. There were these and others intermixed.

"It's just marvelous," Ellen said.

He was very solemn now. "When I'm at home there is no past, no present. I feel I'm suspended in time."

She gazed at him, smiling. "Spooky is as spooky does."

"Actually, when you consider the infinite there is no such thing as time."

"There is at the bus terminal."

That brought him out of it. "Right. I'll order those liverwurst sandwiches."

"Make mine pastrami."

He pressed the button again, and the "footlights" flickered off as the curtain closed over the mural.

The food didn't arrive until almost an hour later, and against the backdrop of rain pouring past the big front window, they sat at one end of the massive oak table munching the sandwiches, Saxon half afraid Marge might have an ESP of her own, somehow sense he was back in town and come barging in.

Ellen, too, seemed tense, her blonde hair brushed to one side of her face; she scarcely looked at him and kept asking about things magic, as though avoiding small, personal talk that might involve either of them. There was a sadness about her; and he, too, seemed to shy from intimacy, instead talked stuffily about magicians past and present.

"In 1889 there was an excellent wizard named Billy Robinson. He had worked with Kellar, and learned enough to go out on his own. Billing himself as 'The Man Of Mystery,' he and his assistant—a pretty, tiny woman, Dot—put on a good show. Come to think of it, he married Dot."

"Do magicians often marry their assistants?"

"It happens. The Great Raymond married lovely, quite beautiful Litzka, and after he died she presented the act. But I'm off the subject."

"Yes, you are," Ellen said, looking past him at the great, rococo room.

"Billy Robinson simply couldn't get an important booking, and then one day he changed his whole façade: he and Dot bought elaborate Chinese costumes, made themselves up Chinese, and had all the stage props rebuilt along Oriental lines. His agent booked them into the Alhambra Theatre in London. They were an instant hit, and in all the years after that, completely lived their Chinese identities on stage and off."

But he saw that her mind was somewhere else, and didn't go on.

They rode back to the Greyhound terminal in excruciating silence, and when it was time to board the bus she didn't kiss him. " 'Bye," she said softly. He watched as the bus pulled out and saw her seated by the window. She was crying, but didn't look up, or wave, and then the bus was gone, its big wheels splashing through a rainswept street; he stood there on the platform, desolate.

But he quickly rationalized: Ellen cried easily. If she had a crush on him, she was young, men would pursue her in Las Vegas, and she'd get over it. Besides, he now had things to do. Call Marge. Start life at home rolling again. Go to the market with her and stock up on groceries. It was a ritual each year when he returned from the tour of theaters. Marge would cook thick rare steaks, they'd drink champagne, she'd spend this first night with him, as usual, and they'd plan the days ahead. That is, if she didn't ask too many questions about why he hadn't wired he was coming. That could lead into one of their famous shouting matches and completely spoil the homecoming.

Yet when he got back to his barn of a place, he didn't call her. It was dark now, rain still coming down, misting the big front window, and he was out of the mood for shopping in a supermarket, had lost his appetite for a thick, rare steak, or champagne. If you're lonely, he told himself, it's deliberate. Pick up the phone.

The telephone rested in its cradle and he did not go near it. Instead walked to the window and stared out through the mist into the night and the rain.

An hour later, he sat at the big table laying out the playing cards he and Ellen had used on the train. He put them down one by one for a game of solitaire, but soon realized he would have to change decks. There was a card missing.

The three of hearts with a fingernail crease on the right-hand corner.

VI

NOW, in the gray of December, the spectrum of his life at home began to reassemble in the usual pattern, bits and pieces of doing and being falling together to make the familiar image: commission for a magazine article on the fallacy of superstition; a lecture in Sacramento before a gathering of Chiefs of Police from around the country; and the simple idyll, taking Marge and her son Marty to a 49'ers–Rams football game, an evening of parlor magic for Marty and his schoolmates; a week-end in Squaw Valley with Marge, marred by a heavy fall of snow, though they had skied anyway. His mood had been odd, there seemed a high, humming unreality in everything he did, as though he were ill of some undiagnosed and incurable malady. It was like a gentle, sad music that never went away, but it didn't show, or affect him. He functioned as usual. So nothing had really changed. He was the same, everything was the same.

"No, you're wrong," Marge said, "you're *not* the same."

The striking redhead sat across the table from him at the Merry-Go-Round bar in the Crown Room on the roof of the Fairmont Hotel, the giant picture windows socked in with fog.

A piano was playing. It was early on a week night and there weren't many patrons. He and Marge had spent the afternoon Christmas shopping in the festively decorated aisles of glittering stores and on impulse had locked the packages in the trunk of his car and came up here for a drink.

He gazed at her now. "I can't imagine what you think is different. We've done the usual December things."

"Yes, I know. But ever since you slipped back into town from Boston there's been something about you. Distant. Aloof."

"You're never going to forgive me for failing to wire I was coming."

Marge sipped her drink, studying him over the rim of the cocktail glass. She had high cheekbones, the cheeks indented, a wide, sensual mouth, deep blue eyes. It was a classic face, the dark, burnished red hair in a page boy bob.

"All right, suppose you *are* the same," she said. "That in itself can be a problem."

It was only now that he recognized the tone. They were going to go into *that* again. It happened once each year. Now it came:

"Tell me the truth, Joe, you're never going to get married again, are you?"

He sat back in his chair listening to the piano.

"*Are* you?" she repeated.

"Yes, I am. How about this weekend? We can fly to Reno."

She stared at him, shocked, and he was amused. That was the last thing she ever expected him to say.

"And no," he went on, "we won't pack Marty off to a boarding school."

That had been a bitter point of contention in last year's discussion.

"But you like living alone."

"It's time I changed."

She simply could not believe it was Saxon saying these things. Then, as if shrewdly analyzing his motives: "Oh, I see, you feel it's an obligation. A great debt of some kind that you owe me and now you're ready to settle the account."

"If that's the case, how come I didn't feel it last year, the year before, or the year before that?"

She was embarrassed, at a loss. "It—just caught up with you. You're afraid you've hurt me. That I'm a damaged human being. That's the way you think. Well, I'm not damaged. I'm fine. Give your conscience a rest."

"Marge, what the hell is it you want?"

"Most of all for you to be happy." She was hop, skipping and jumping, looking around as if for a cue card that would show her what to say next. "You'd be miserable married to me, and you know it. Besides, where would the three of us live? Up in that museum of yours?"

"We'll get a house in Carmel."

Her incredulity became even more acute. "You'd give up the loft?"

"No, I'll keep it. Commute back and forth."

"That means I wouldn't see you any more than I do now."

"Must I give up every last scrap of my privacy?"

"You don't have to give up anything. I don't want to marry you any more. You waited too long." She had tears in her eyes, and he sat in stunned silence as she went on: "I'm sorry, Joe. I was being a bitch. I thought you'd refuse and that'd give me the out I needed. Those old platitudes about security, a boy needs a father—but you see, you trapped me."

Piano playing softly; fog shrouding the windows.

He was sinking out of sight.

He tried to talk, and couldn't, the words drowned in his throat.

Crying harder, she said: "Darling, I don't want to hurt *you* either. God knows I don't want to hurt you. I've loved you. There were times I loved you so desperately I wanted to die."

"You loved me."

"I still do," she said, "and always will. You're good, you're kind, gentle—"

"No, I've been selfish."

"—But we're wasted. It's over."

Looking past her, he said, "Don't blame yourself. I should have married you long ago. When a man lives alone with himself too long what finally happens is he falls off the end of the earth." Gazing at her now, offering a handkerchief. That dear, classic face tear-streaked. "But I don't really understand. What brought it to a head here, now, with only five more shopping days till Christmas?"

The sad piano.

I think I have a toothache.

God, that fog.

"While you were out on tour, I met a man—"

So things were changed, after all. It wasn't the same. Nothing was the same.

He took her home.

In the car again, swirling fog so thick he could scarcely make out street lights, the radio was playing an old Bing Crosby record, *White Christmas*.

Numb.

Stick a pin in and see if it hurts.

Look, it's just your pride.

A foggy night in San Francisco town . . .

What else is new?

In the hall outside the door of his loft apartment he heard the telephone ringing, but by the time he got in and picked up the receiver it had stopped. The line was dead.

He put the cold, black instrument down and looked at it.

Let's call up a lot of people and have a party.

The chiefs of police in different cities around the country.
They'll drop law enforcement and fly right out.
You can do magic tricks for them.
He walked over to the baroque bar, picked up a bottle and
poured half a glass of whiskey.
Atta boy. Shoot yourself down.
The trouble was it took quite a while, and after he had
tucked himself into the immense bed, he was dead to the world.
Almost. Hours later (or was it only minutes?) the telephone
began to ring again. One ring, two, then three. Dimly conscious.
Four rings, five. Awake, groping. Six, seven. Up, stumbling over
his shoes. Eight rings. The black, blunt thing shrilling in the
darkness.
"Hello?"
Hum of the dial tone.
She had hung up.
Plopping himself in a chair, fumbling with a cigarette,
lighting it, head fuzzy. She? Why, necessarily, was it a she?
Anybody might have called. An urgent case for the brilliant
psychic detective, for instance. At this hour? All right, what
hour is it? He got up and although the blue night light was on
had to carefully navigate his way to the bedside table to pick up
his wrist watch. He flicked on his lighter. Four minutes after
twelve. The telephone had rung at midnight. Only a psychic
practitioner of black art, he thought, would attach significance
to that. The witching hour.
That brought his mind back to the lady who had for such a
long time been his own private witch.
"While you were on tour—"
He consoled himself: be honest, you didn't truly love her.
She was a lovely, convenient habit. You rat. I'd have married
her, though. What's wrong with a permanent habit as nice as
that one? But love? Not since Helen, and I was too young in
those days to know that love, like the supernatural, doesn't

really exist. Exquisite illusion, pleasure-dependence, yes, but each human being is dark and alone within himself. If not, why had Marge been able to so casually change *her* pleasure-depend ence?

Saxon, the great philosopher.

Crap.

Back to bed, old buddy.

In bed, head sinking back on the nice, soft pillow.

Wonder how the kid is doing in Las Vegas?

Got a job right away, I'm sure.

A single rose in a slim vase, and a dark, wet wooded glade flashing by the dining car window.

Our Father Who art in heaven . . .

Then he was asleep again, and at three A.M. two Hal lowe'en goblins came out of the woodwork and set up the nightmare: they informed him he now possessed one facet in the true art of black magic, then ran off. And he dreamed an alarm clock was ringing. He reached over to turn it off and as he touched it, it disappeared, still ringing, the sound receding in the distance. He got up quickly, stooped for his slippers, but the moment he made contact they, too, went hurtling off into a void. He shrewdly deduced his right hand was the conductor of the vanishing and thereafter tried to employ his left hand for everything, though from time to time forgot, nervously picking up three different cigarettes that went *poof* out of sight; and later, in the shower, when the water started getting too hot vanished the faucet, water continuing to stream out of the overhead nozzle and by then almost scalding him so that he adiosed the shower door, trying to get out of the stall, the steaming shower still running, its glass door completely gone He had a difficult time dressing with his left hand. No matter what he tried to do, it went wrong. It took him a good half hour to tie his shoe laces, and by now he was terrified because he knew damn well there *was* no such thing as true magic, and something had to be wrong. His life had gone askew. He could not explain why things kept disappearing, and he had no control, could not command the objects to reappear. It was as if a sorcerer's curse had been put on him. Growing increasingly flustered, he knew he had to tell somebody of the awful power he possesssed, and made the mistake of reaching for the telephone with his right hand. Gone. The headless cord lay at his feet. This somehow frightened him more than the disappearance of any of the other items. Poltergeists? No, they didn't vanish objects, merely hurled them around the room. He moved to the door, trembling now, and just barely caught himself before clutching the knob with his right hand. He opened the door with his left hand and ran to the elevator. On the street, he waved down a cab and once inside gave Marge's address. She knew him better than anyone and might suggest some solution. God knew he was incapable of thinking at this point. At the very least Marge would be sympathetic to the problem. As the cab sped through the streets he sat tensely holding up his right hand, much as though it had the plague. In front of Marge's place, it was awkward trying to dig money out of his right hand pocket with his left hand. The driver kept staring at him, and at his right hand, held like a man taking an oath. Marge answered the door, and though he warned her not to touch that now stiff and quivering magic hand, she thought he had injured it, and saying, "Here, let me see it," touched it before he could stop her and vanished. He opened his mouth, trying to scream, but couldn't, no sound would come, and then he was back on the street again, berserk, a madman. Nothing more mattered. He saw a particularly ugly old office building, the appearance of which had blighted the neighborhood for years. Brushing by a policeman who was staring at the way he was weaving crazily up the street, he rushed to the building and vindictively laid his right hand on the cornerstone. Instant vacant lot. The cop gaped, then numbly, but instinctively bound by duty, even if by

God, it was the end of the world, moved up to Saxon saying, idiotically, that what he had done was against the law. "So is this," Saxon said, and put his hand on the officer's shoulder. Empty space stood where the policeman had been, and after that Saxon ran amuck. He vanished a cable car including all the people aboard. I wonder, he thought, if I can make the Golden Gate Bridge disappear? He sprinted down Market Street, vanishing people left and right as startled bystanders fainted, screamed, ran, fell to their knees, or simply shut their eyes to blot out something they could not have witnessed. Saxon was still running when the oblivion of sleep wiped out the nightmare. However, from then on, stirring restlessly, he tried to grasp at a sound he knew he had heard. That alarm clock that kept ringing as it receded in the distance? Yes, that alarm clock. That alarm clock.

He woke at ten in the morning, deeply depressed. While shaving, he remembered the nightmare, almost in detail, and, a man who believed in signs, if not from the beyond, from somewhere, analyzed the dream. His life-long pursuit in search of a true magic. Well, it had been thrown at him and it was a horror. But the deepest meaning of the nightmare was that everything and everybody he touched in life were disappearing. He had all but cleaved himself of human contact in search of what? A foolish, unfulfilled, unfulfillable quest into forbidden darkness. It was time he faced himself. What an awful thing to have to face yourself.

But over coffee and soft-boiled eggs, he did. What group enjoyed magic more than any other? Children. It was a child's game of pretend. Lovely, haunting, mystifying, it beckoned its slender wand: come with me to the land of never. As a child, magic had been his first love, and it had endured, but now perhaps it was time to end that long affair. He was no longer a child, though clearly he had lived as one, selfishly hoarding his bag of astounding tricks. Watch. See me perform my miracles. A grown-up child. A show-off. And to justify such total dedication to nonsense making yourself believe there is more to the illusion than mirrors. There is a reality out there, a truth in the unknown, and by persevering you will find it.

The egg cup was empty, the coffee cold, when he finally seriously considered giving up magic and all its devious cloaks. No more theater tours, no more performances anywhere; sell the props, wipe out every last trace of legerdemain. If ignorant people persist in believing in haunted houses, expose the hoax for a fee. He could live comfortably and even amuse himself following that singular endeavor.

The Great Saxon, finest magician in the world, smiled inwardly.

He had sought almost a whole lifetime to reach the unattainable, and now that futile chase was over.

You're no different from anybody else living out his time on this earth. You can't find a secret knowledge that doesn't exist.

An hour later, he was deep in the realities of day to day existence. It was the holiday season, and he knew he couldn't endure being in San Francisco with Marge just across town; too many memories of Christmases past; and besides Marge, he'd be carrying a torch for the magic he had decided to divorce. The answer was to go to some interesting faraway place and for a time at least become involved in and with it. But where? Go where? Hong Kong. A city he had always wanted to visit. Christmas Day and New Year's Eve in Hong Kong. That intrigued, excited him, picked up his spirits.

He called Pan Am and found there was a flight leaving at two that afternoon. He'd have to hurry, but he could make it. His passport was in order. He thought of Billy Robinson and his wife Dot who had lived so many years in Chinese makeup, on stage and off, but had never been to China. Well, he'd see it for them.

At the bustling airport, he felt happy, buoyant. A whole new life lay before him. He picked up his ticket, checked his baggage through to the plane, and went into the bar for a drink. Though he seldom drank in the daytime, now it didn't matter. He could relax on the plane.

Through a loudspeaker, a soft, feminine voice was announcing imminent arrivals, departures and summoning tardy outgoing passengers to the ticket desk. Saxon was on his second Manhattan, listening to that, and to the babble of voices here in the cocktail lounge when something like a red light began to flash on and off in his mind.

Christ, what's that?

Then he heard the whisper of her voice: "Joe . . . Joe . . ."

He looked around, but Ellen wasn't there.

It had been Ellen's voice.

Through the loudspeaker: "Pan American Flight 714, departing for Honolulu and Hong Kong now boarding at Gate 128."

"Joe . . ."

ESP.

It electrified him.

At the Pan Am desk, he cancelled out his ticket.

"Sir, it's too late to get your luggage off the plane."

"Doesn't matter. Fly it back from Honolulu."

"Yes, sir."

Alarm clock ringing at three in the morning?

It had been the telephone.

Ellen.

VII

THOUGH THE OFFICE was brightly lighted, garish blobs of red, blue, purple and green neon seemed to splash like streaks of paint against the shiny glass of the second floor windows; images depicting race horses, dice, a poker hand, signs that read *Casino, 7–11 Club, Lucky Horseshoe* glowed in the darkness high above the teeming, mad gambling jungle below. But those same windows shut out the noises on the street, and the air was blue and putrefied with stale cigar smoke, Turk sitting behind his vast, circular desk: bald, obscene, the eyes of more than five hundred pretty young women looking at him from glossy eight-by-ten pictures that covered the entire four walls from ceiling to floor.

Turk had been searching through a file, but now he pushed it aside and looked up at Saxon.

"Hey, I don't need this. I remember her now. Kook, ain't she? Real ding-a-ling."

"Where do I find her?"

"Hold your horses, Mr. Saxon." Turk relit a dead stogie.

"Let me tell you the way she came on." It was evidently a story the booking agent relished.

Saxon had declined an invitation to sit in the hope he could get out of here as quickly as possible. But now, standing near the desk, there was something in Turk's tone that bothered him.

"All right. How did she come on?"

"I book dancers, strictly nothing but dancers and showgirls all up and down the Strip. Oh, now and then I may dally with a little sideline—" He winked lewdly.

"Never mind the sideline."

"Well, the point is," Turk said, "I don't book acts. Haven't got a franchise for that. Acts big or small. Acts, that's something else." He was having difficulty getting the dead stogie going again "And the thing is, *she* knew that. This—what's her name?"

"Ellen Hayes."

"Yeah. So she walks in here wearing a coat. That's okay, lot of 'em do. Have leotards on underneath, anyway little enough so I can get a gander at their legs and their tits to see if they measure up. Takes more than a pretty face, you know. The chassis has to come with it."

"She wore a coat."

Turk nodded, his mirror-like bald head reflecting a kaleidoscope of light from outside. "And she was carrying some kind of a folding table. She opened it and set it down. *Then* she took off the coat."

When Ellen took off the cloth coat, Turk thought somebody must have been putting him on. Though it fit her perfectly, she was wearing a man's formal tailcoat, the traditional magician's garb, and shorts of the same dark, satin material. She had on long silk stockings, and a white blouse with a black bow tie. An instant later she popped open a high, silk top hat which she put on, tilting it saucily over one eye. Next, a thin black wand appeared as if from out of nowhere.

"What are you supposed to be?"

Poised there on high heels, the stance of her shapely legs a study in symmetry that even Turk could not help but admire, she said simply, "I do magic," and before the words were out a deck of cards had materialized in her hands.

Turk started to get up, but quickly sat back down as she sailed one of the cards toward him, then a second and a third. They circled his head, Turk twisting his neck to look up at them, then returned to Ellen's waiting hands. For just a moment she seemed to fumble with the deck, but presently was performing a series of conventional sleight-of-hand card tricks.

Turk began to fume. "Will you explain to me what you think you're doing?"

"Yes, sir, I'm auditioning for you."

He tried not to be impressed as eight cards in a row seemingly vanished from her right hand and immediately reappeared in her left.

"Auditioning for what, for Christ's sake?"

"I thought you might place me in the lounge at one of the smaller clubs. I know some of those lounge shows have three or four different acts, and—"

"I don't book acts."

"I've tried for the last three days to get an agent who does," Ellen said, "but—"

"But they laughed you out of their offices."

Ellen stopped performing. She was flustered, nervous, and so discouraged that it galled. "I've just come off an engagement with the world's greatest magician."

"All those creeps claim they're the world's greatest."

She bristled. "This man is. And he is *not* a creep."

Turk had thought for a moment she was going to assault him physically, and when he realized she wasn't, got up from behind the desk, walked over to her, and with a cigar jammed in his mouth, stood there looking her up and down as if trying to suppress a giggle.

"Where'd you get those freak-out duds?"

"I bought them before I left home."

"When was that?"

"Almost three years ago."

"Ever work your own magic act?"

"No, sir."

"Then what makes you think you can come to a place like Las Vegas and—"

"You could at least let me *try*." Her voice was weighted by unseen tears. "I'm sure you know enough people. If you wanted to arrange it, you could."

"What would there be in it for me?"

"A ten percent commission," she snapped.

He made a circle around her, inspecting the coattails, pulling at them, shoving the high silk hat further over her face, and now she was conscious of the faces in those glossy pictures all around the room, each of which had been photographed in such a way that the eyes always looked at you. She had noticed them at once, pretending not to, but now it seemed they had suddenly become inescapable.

She made one last attempt. "You could bill me as 'The Magic Lady.' "

"Not interested."

She reached for her cloth street coat, but he spun her around.

"You a dancer?"

"Yes." Dully.

"You want a job?"

"Yes, I'm afraid I do."

"Then take off that monkey suit coat and let me have a look at you."

She hesitated, then removed the magician's coat. Her ripe, bra-less breasts poked out the material of the white blouse, but when Turk stepped toward her she plucked the cigar from his mouth, reversed it, the burning end threatening his face. Turk was in no mood for games. He took back the cigar and returned to his desk.

"There's an opening for a pony in the chorus line at Rainbow's End. A hundred and twenty-five a week."

She squeezed the tophat shut, embarrassed that she had brought it, the folding table, or any of the other paraphernalia.

"Who do I ask for?"

"Ned Barnes. I'll call and tell him you're coming."

Ned Barnes wasn't in when Saxon arrived at Rainbow's End, and since the showgirls were already in the theater dressing room making up, he decided to wait in the casino's large, crowded lounge. There was a stage above the long bar and what amounted to an almost continuous show was on.

The lounge was adjacent to the gambling pit: several dice tables, all in action, eight where black jack was being played, four roulette tables, and two of Faro, banked by row after row of slot machines, their clanging ceaseless. Here in the lounge there were tables and booths where the wives of preoccupied, high-rolling husbands could sit, sip a drink, watch whatever act was in progress before again gathering up their rolls of nickels, dimes, quarters and half dollars for another frantic session with those cold, metal, one-armed bandits.

Saxon watched the act on stage. It was a trio of talented

name musicians but even with a battery of mikes to amplify the sound it was difficult to appreciate them over the din and clatter coming from the pit: dice hitting the backboard, excited shouts of players, the drone of the croupiers, "Seven, seven the winner. Pay the front line. Same lucky shooter coming out again. Get your bets down. Who wants insurance? Ee-o or any. Eight. Eight, the number, eight the point. Make eight the hard way . . ."

But he concentrated on the stage above the bar and instead of the trio saw Ellen, in cottail and tophat. He had thought her pushy, and in a way she had been, yet she had never once divulged she wanted to be a lady magician. A confession of that kind would have embarrassed her in the presence of someone she considered the foremost exponent of magic. So there was, after all, a shy side to her nature. There were secrets she had kept locked up. In the fear of being laughed at? Didn't she know *he* wouldn't have laughed? But had she, in fact, known him that well? When had he ever given her a chance to know him at all? He with his own dark secrets and cold exterior. He hadn't once shared any of his true, deep self with her. He had wanted to, but the subconscious buffer against pain and hurt, the fear of being laughed at himself, had stopped him. Hadn't she said she was only "using" him to get a free train ride to San Francisco? For a single instant there in that dank dressing room in Boston he had doubted that, felt it was a defense she had manufactured, but afterward, perhaps because of his own self-doubts, he had accepted that as her motive for traveling with him.

Ellen up on that stage performing her simple magic. The art of sailing cards out and causing them to return to her. That, surely, had taken an infinity of practice. It was the trick Thurston had perfected in the summer of 1898 before a saloon full of drunken miners somewhere in the wilds of Montana. It was difficult, complicated, done with what a magician could only hope were invisible threads. No wonder Ellen had seemed to fumble after demonstrating that lovely illusion for Turk. Undoubtedly the threads had become tangled. It was an elaborate trick and Saxon would have to scold her for exhibiting it at the outset of the ill-fated audition instead of saving it for the climactic feat it was.

And now, still staring at that stage above the bar that he didn't really see, he realized he *had* to find her here, be with her, talk to her; soothe away whatever alarm had projected her call to him.

He smiled, suddenly happy. ESP worked for them. She'd proven it far better than a simple breakfast menu in the dining car of a speeding train. Kid, listen, we'll discuss it, practice it, test it. Somebody at last, he thought, who *wants* to talk about and live the same pretty dream that I've tried to hold in my heart all these years. God, that alone is a new frontier in a life that has been corroding away under its own self-imposed burden of loneliness.

Impatient now, and exhilarated, he paid for his drink and returned to the reservation desk. No, Mr. Barnes still had not returned. They would page Saxon when he did. But it didn't really matter. He'd be seeing her soon. He sauntered through the gambling pit, and in a gay mood, approached a dollar slot machine. He had seven silver dollars concealed in the lining of his suit coat. Like certain magicians who were always "on," he, too, was often on, or anyway prepared to be, and the lining of his suit coats had been specially sewn with inner pleats, pockets and niches that held the secrets of his trade.

As though unaware there was anyone else in the crowded room he solemnly lifted his arm up and seemingly plucked a silver dollar out of the air. He put it in the machine and pulled the handle. Wheels spun behind a glass pane and stopped to show a lemon, a bar and an orange. Nothing. Saxon again reached up, a silver dollar trickled down from nowhere and perched between his fingertips, three people now gaping at him. He paid no attention, played the dollar, lost, and found still another in the smoky blue atmosphere. The crowd of onlookers had increased to seven or eight, and then genuine magic occurred. Three bells flashed behind the square of glass and sixteen silver dollars clattered loudly into the metal maw at the bottom of the machine.

Saxon picked them up, appeared to toss three into the air from whence they had come, and carried the rest to a change girl who gave him bills. Through all of this, the corner of his eye had been on a long queue of people waiting to enter the theater. They were now going inside. He walked past them directly to the maitre d', and appearing to shake the man's hand, deposited the money in his palm.

"Are you alone, sir?"

"Temporarily," Saxon said.

Though the theater was sold out for the first show, Saxon was taken to a ringside table. There was always something available provided one performed the correct ritual. The dining room–theater was filling rapidly, and Saxon ordered a drink, then sat back and waited for the curtains to open on the big stage.

When a platform slowly elevated from the pit bringing musicians into view he found himself almost a-tremble with excitement in anticipation of seeing the kid again. Then his anxiety complex manifested itself. What had impelled her to try and reach him by telephone the one whole, long night? And then, finally, the next day, by ESP? She had said on the train that perhaps ESP only worked at a time of crisis. He was positive he had received her telepathic message. *Was* there a crisis? Surely it had to be minor. Intense loneliness, for instance, sending out little cries for help. But that could be assuaged. It was nothing to fret over. Not now. Not here.

The orchestra began to play, lights were dimming, and now the curtains swept open on a line of girls clad in jeweled V-shaped tights, skimpy, jeweled bras, and dazzling hairbands, dancing in exact precision timing. Willowy wisps of other curtains parted upstage, revealing tall, lovely showgirls, each on graduating pedestals, arms outstretched, striking the pose of statues, their large breasts bare. Soft, colored lights revolved, all hues, the music picking up in tempo, and Saxon sat tensely, looking from face to face. But the lithe, graceful little dancers were twisting, turning, constantly moving, and it was legs you saw, shapely, naked legs were accentuated. Legs. The faces now in shadow, now out; the dance growing more frantic, sensuous, the girls squealing, legs lifting high, legs kicking in unison. One by one, one at a time, the faces. Concentrate on their faces. One of them belongs to Ellen.

None of them belonged to Ellen.

When he was absolutely sure she was not up there on the Rainbow's End stage he left in mid-show and returned to the reservation desk. Ned Barnes was still absent. He was the only person on the premises authorized to discuss show personnel. No, there was no room telephone number listed for Ellen Hayes. If she had been here, she had checked out.

Saxon wandered through the gambling pit, waiting for the show in the theater to break. Certainly one of the ponies would know Ellen's whereabouts.

He had learned on past visits that this and other big Strip casinos had a clause in the contract that the girls in the chorus line frequent a small bar at the end of the room between shows. Ostensibly so customers could buy them a drink, get acquainted, and if they got lucky—. However, it hadn't worked out quite that flagrantly. Time had proven the fever of gambling possesses men to the point where nothing else, not even sex, is important. The few persistent lounge lizards that pestered the pretty showgirls were easily put off. Actually, that turn of events frustrated the normal, sexy young females. On week nights when business was slack they were bored to distraction, and a really eligible male in their midst had often ignited cat fights.

Saxon was seated at that small bar when the music in the theater reached a crescendo, then ended; a few minutes later the girls came trailing out, wearing street clothes, but still in stage makeup. The first one, with ebony, straight black hair, shot Saxon a look: as though she felt he had stopped at this little way-station bar by mistake. But mistake or not, she plunked herself down on a stool beside him.

"Hi," she said.

"Hi. May I buy you a drink?"

She nodded. "I can use a drink."

By the time the drink was served the bar was ringed with the doll-like ponies.

"My name's Carla," the girl with the ebony hair said, "I'm half Indian, and I'm drinking fire water, so watch out."

"Actually, Carla, I'm trying to locate a girl who worked here in the chorus line."

"Oh." Disappointed.

"Ellen Hayes."

"Oh. *Her.*"

"You know her?"

Carla nodded. "Broke her contract. They don't like that in this town. Funny the way it happened. There's this creep that comes in here. He's a magician of some kind. Has an act in town. Bills himself as 'Professor Marvelous.'" She sighed, sipped her drink. "How corny can you get?"

"Not much more than that."

"His big come-on is he'll hire you as his assistant. We all

know his assistant on stage just happens to be his ever-lovin' wife, but a couple of the girls fell for that stupid line and all they got was laid. He's nothin' but a stinkin' little coyote," she went on, "a coyote is—"

"I know, a small-time wolf."

"Yep. Well, he fed the same line to Ellen, but something funny happened on the way to that room he rents here for his extracurricular playmates. She didn't go, and he actually *did* hire her as his assistant."

"How the hell'd she manage that?"

"He found out she'd just been assistant to a really great magician, and man, did he ever get charged up. Big wheel named Joe Saxon. Hell, even *I've* heard of him, and I'm just a dumb Indian broad."

"You said 'Professor Marvelous' had a wife as an assistant. How could he fire her and hire Ellen?"

"Who knows?"

"You say he works here in town?"

"Mm-huh. At the Golden Mirage. Little dump of a motel–casino on the outskirts. Other side of the railroad tracks."

"Thanks, Carla."

"Case I see her, who'll I say wanted to know?"

He stood up, paid the bill, then said, "Joe Saxon."

❧VIII❧

IT WAS a forlorn-looking place in an abandoned part of town, and even as he approached on the two-lane road, it looked incredible, looming out of the drab darkness, indeed like a mirage: all the sparkling lights of the motel and the adjoining casino, a green neon wheel of chance turning in the black sky, and the bright glow of orange letters: *Golden Mirage*. A place for the desperate and the lonely, Saxon thought. The casinos along the rich, gaudy Vegas Strip imposed invisible restrictions; one could walk into a Rainbow's End wearing old, baggy, perhaps soiled clothes, a hayseed look on his face, and there would be no stir, no murmur, yet somehow he would be gone less than fifteen minutes later; dowdy vacationing tourists from the mid-West could enter, sweaty, ill-clad, their trailer or camper truck parked outside, people obviously on a budget, gawking at the sights, kids in tow, and it would turn out they might as well have stayed in the revolving door that would sweep them out again.

However, here at the Golden Mirage it was obvious anybody, just anybody could walk in and lose his money.

The casino was small, just two crap tables, three of blackjack, one of roulette, a wheel of chance, and of course cadres of slot machines. The patrons who wandered about were as sleazy as the background, yet equally as possessed with the feverish excitement of a gambling pit as those who inhabited the far more plush palaces of pleasure.

There was a stage above the bar, a quintet of musicians playing love songs. The motel registration desk was also crowded into one corner of the room. The clerk was a visibly nervous young man with a trace of acne.

"Sir, I am sorry to tell you, Professor Marvelous is still in his room."

"Why are you so sorry about it?"

"He and his assistant were due in the dressing room twenty minutes ago."

"His assistant?"

"Yes, sir, his wife."

"What happened to—"

"You mean that beautiful girl he worked with for the past three nights? I don't know. All he said was that she was fired and his wife Dana is back."

" 'Professor Marvelous'? He *does* have a name."

"Yes, sir. Dekker. George Dekker."

"What room are he and his wife in?"

"Twenty. That's upstairs. Please ask them to get down here. I can hold the show up for a little while, but not long. It's our big attraction."

"Oh? You're also in charge of the entertainment?"

The nervous, fidgety young man nodded. "We don't have a very large staff. But I'm *not* the boss. If he doesn't come on with that act I could wind up with two broken arms."

"Things are that bad?"

"No, sir, not quite, but things *have* been so lousy lately you wouldn't believe it."

"Room 20?"

"Yes, at the head of the stairs, off the balcony."

Loud, angry voices were emitting from inside the door of Room 20, and there on the balcony, Saxon hesitated, then listened.

"Forget it, you dirty, stinking, nothing two-timing son-of-a-bitch."

Obviously wife Dana.

"God damn it, I said you're going to appear."

"Hell I am, lover-boy."

"You want to ruin me?"

"What have you ever done but ruin *me?*"

"Maybe you'd rather be back behind a soda fountain!"

"Anywhere."

"You know I can't go on without an assistant."

"Excuse me while I laugh."

"Don't make me scream at you like this. Don't make me plead. I don't have to tell you the show has to go on."

"Oh, God, don't give me *that* old hocus-pocus baloney."

"Look, damn you, I'm on my knees."

"How's the view from down there?"

"*Dana—*"

"Do a solo."

"You're perfectly aware I can't work half those tricks without help."

"Darling, try it. You'd have a whole new career—as a comic."

"*God damn you!*"

"Do the flowers-sprouting-out-of-your-ear bit."

"Honey, I'm *begging.*"

"Honey, I'm deaf. And I'm leaving. Tonight."

"You *can't.*"

"No, George, don't stand up. You look better on your knees."

"I told you why I hired Ellen Hayes."

"You were going to get rich." Derisive.

"I'm sick of scratching month after month for just enough to keep us going."

"From now on all you'll have to scratch is yourself."

"All right, walk out if you want—"

"I want."

"—*Get* a divorce, who the hell cares? But don't leave me high and dry in the middle of an engagement."

"Where'd you leave me three days ago?"

"I've told you repeatedly—"

"Listen, Professor Marvelous, as far as I'm concerned you're all out of marvels. I stood by while you were on the make for every little tart in town. I knew you had a rented room somewhere for those indoor pleasures. But I stuck, idiot that I am, I stood by. I put on my black net stockings and appeared up there on stage in that micro-skirt and showed off my cute little ass to those crummy slobs in your audience. Which do you think pleased them most? Your little magic fish bowl with fish swimming in it or my little magic can? Don't answer because you know the answer. I've taken it and taken it and taken it with you and your floozies. But when you move one of them in next door and bump me off the stage because, quotes She appeared with The Great Saxon and I need the kind of publicity that'll bring, unquotes, that cut it."

"Just at least do tonight's show."

"Hand me my dress, Stupid." Silence, then: "No, not that itty bitty micro-skirt."

"Either you put that on or I'll—"

There was a sound of cloth being ripped.

"You *bitch!*"

A scuffle of feet, a smothered scream.

Saxon pounded on the door.

Silence inside. Heavy breathing.

"Open up," Saxon said.

"Who is it?"

"Open the door, Mr. Dekker."

The door opened just an inch, but Saxon shoved against it, throwing George Dekker back.

Inside, Saxon saw Dekker's face drained white, his hands shaking, bulging eyes now slowly receding back into their sockets. Dana stood clad in high heels, silk stockings, black transparent scanty-panties, and a see-through bra, her nipples looking very pink through the black mesh. She was no more than five foot two, dark-complexioned, big, flashing black eyes, and silky dark hair that trickled down her back. Here, in the first moment seeing Saxon, her hands were clutching at a red welt on her neck, and she made no move to cover herself. A costume skirt lay torn at her feet.

Saxon closed the door, taking in Dekker again, a small nondescript man whose face looked as though it had been molded out of bread dough, little seams showing, and those features were hindered, not helped, by a tiny, thin, pencil-line moustache. Clad in a magician's tailcoat, he was the living cliché of what a jaded audience expected when the curtain rang up on a magic act in some fleabitten little hall. Professor Marvelous. Saxon could envision his exaggerated stage flourish, the inevitable deck of trick playing cards, yes, even petunias sprouting from his ear, and it sickened him, made him ashamed of his cherished profession.

The "professor" was peering at Saxon.

"I've seen you somewhere."

"I imagine you have."

He looked at his wife. "Dana, for God's sake, put something on."

"Up yours," she said, then looked at Saxon. "He tried to kill me."

Had Saxon interrupted an act of murder? The thought chilled him. Who had chosen *him* to mediate the life or death of others? What odd quirk of a predestined fate had placed him outside the door at that woefully correct moment?

"I was trying to shake some sense into her," Dekker said.

He was nursing his deft, magician's fingers, seeming worried they might be bruised to the point of impairing the manipulation of sleight-of-hand.

"Mister," Dana said, "would you like to see my cute little fanny? He's been making a living off it for years."

"Damn you," Professor Marvelous shrieked, "he thinks you mean I'm a pimp." He turned to Saxon. "I'm a magician. She's my—"

Staring at Saxon now, Dana interrupted: "Who the living hell *are* you?"

"Joe Saxon."

Professor Marvelous gaped, suddenly in great awe. But was it also fear that seemed to make deeper seams in his bread-dough face?

"The Great Saxon," he said. "Of course."

The petite Dana wasn't quite as celebrity conscious. "He's come for his girl." She ran to a table, picked up a prop high silk hat, and pulling hard with both hands, jammed it down over her husband's ears. "He wants his girl back, Stupid." She was shouting, half crying. "Which leads up to a real peachy question. Just where the hell is she? That's something even *I'd* like to know."

The professor's pencil-line moustache looked like wriggling rabbit whiskers as he tried to wedge the hat off his face. "It's show time. Don't you realize it's show time?"

Saxon jerked the hat off the wretched Mr. Dekker. "Where is she?"

"Mr. Saxon, surely *you* know what it means to miss a performance."

"He probably made a pass," Dana said, "and she let him have it and took off. See that bruise on his cheek bone?" She pointed. "Right there. He's got it covered with makeup."

Saxon detected a small, bluish swelling under the pancake makeup.

Professor Marvelous was now in such a state of nerves he could not bring himself to look at Saxon. He paced up and down in a fit of growing agitation, and unpleasant musty sweat of fear oozing from every pore in his body.

"Yes. Ellen Hayes took off. I don't know where she is."

Dana said: "Why don't you give him that crap you gave me about the man with the clubfoot and how much money the two of you were going to make?"

Saxon's whole body stiffened.

The magician's convention in Miami. An old man with a clubfoot limping over to the bar, his wheezy voice a patronizing whine. "Mr. Saxon, my name is Eli Wheeler. I own a magic shop in East St. Louis. It will be the proudest moment of my life if I am permitted to say I met you and shook your hand." And Saxon had clasped that clammy hand.

He lifted Dekker up from under his armpits and shoved him, legs dangling, against the wall.

"Tell me about this clubfoot."

"I lied. I lied to her. There isn't any character like that."

"Is the name Eli Wheeler?"

"No, I don't know anybody like that. I made the whole thing up."

Dana moaned, half screamed. Despite everything she had evidently still clung to a slim hope that the excuse Dekker had invented for associating with Ellen was true.

Saxon still had the little magician pinned against the wall like a fly, wondering, with horror, who was goading him into such a frenzy.

the monthly meeting of afficionados-of-legerdemain, and Eli Wheeler had a special treat for them: ancient film clips of magic acts where the great masters of the craft (many of them now dead) could be seen "actually, they, themselves, in person" performing their "world-celebrated" illusions.

Eli Wheeler sat on a high stool near a small, portable screen, making that spiel, his hawkish face intense with excitement, darting eyes defying anyone to be critical of his elaborate descriptions. But no one was. The atmosphere was church-like, hushed, as though this were the prelude of a sacred ritual.

And to the motley collection of "afficionados" it was exactly that. If magicians as a whole were devoted to their profession, the hangers-on, much like mesmerized worshippers in a fan club, more than matched it in their pitiable reverence for the wizards who conjured up mystifying illusions. They literally offered up their one-dimensional souls to be burned like incense.

The man who had informed Saxon what the meeting was about had scarcely glanced at him, was in fact irritated that he might miss one precious word of Eli Wheeler's preamble, and before Saxon could speak again the lights had gone out, the phosphorous faces of magic shop rubber masks dangling ghoulishly above: a leering skull, Frankenstein, hideous ogres, grotesque witches. The projectionist was ready, and the grainy, uneven, silent black-and-white film flashed on the small screen.

Saxon stood pressed between afficionados, both male and female, watching their faces: absorbed, enraptured, and looking, he thought, like imbecile death masks in the thrall of orgasm. They didn't cough, scarcely breathed; all cigarettes had been put out for the duration of the filmed ceremony to their gods.

"Now, there you see The Magnificent Kashi," Eli Wheeler intoned. "Kashi, himself, in person." He kept repeating "in person" as though the Hindu master had come off the screen and joined them here. "*Kashi* slicing a woman in half with one powerful stroke of a Damascus sword."

Saxon freely acknowledged Kashi's illusion was a superior feat, for his "victim" (a young woman assistant) was not covered, either by a curtain or so much as a pass with a cape, and the blade seemingly slashed through her middle. Audiences had gasped, women screamed, fainted; and even here in the shop, the old, faded film sent an audible chill through the onlookers. The secret of how it was done had never been divulged. Kashi had taken it to the grave with him.

What Saxon resented was Eli Wheeler's implication that the body of the "hypnotized" woman had truly been severed, then bloodlessly mended back together.

"There, you *see*," the clubfoot was saying, "no trick there." He seemed to be grinding his teeth, and again his furtive eyes darted out, probing, scanning the faces of those in the dark.

Now there was another magician on the screen. He shot a gun at a woman and to demonstrate the bullet had made a hole through her, drew a ribbon back and forth, from backbone to stomach; to Saxon's mind, the manner in which this not-quite-illusion had been achieved was easily discernible. However, there was not so much as a stir in the standee group.

"She, too, was of course hypnotized," Wheeler said, his clubfoot hooked on one rung of the stool. "She felt nothing, and in that hypnotic state, the wound healed within minutes."

That was too much. Saxon studied the faces around him. Surely there would be a smile or two. Hadn't Eli Wheeler made a joke? Wasn't that gross exaggeration meant to be funny, something to lighten his patter as he commented on the film? But to his horror, Saxon found acceptance on most of the faces.

He had never before been this close to a clique of magic fanatics, and was appalled at their naiveté. Or was it that? Was it that deep down they *wanted* to believe the unreal, just as he had once on another level? He saw they were revelling almost obscenely in the goings-on. And then he thought he detected another reason for their trance-like captivity. He observed Eli Wheeler's face closely, watched his eyes, and felt he knew the trick: on a minor scale, the same kind of mass hypnosis Saxon himself employed on stage. The clubfoot was holding the afficionados in a cataleptic state.

But Saxon rejected that theory, too, at least in part. A fiery evangelist could evoke the same power over an audience of thousands packed in a single auditorium. In certain sections of the South, Holy Rollers gyrated in frenzy at the sound of a voice instructing them on heaven and hell and it mattered to them not at all how they achieved their mindless euphoria.

A performance of the Hindu Rope Trick was now flickering across the screen. The magician was not Kashi, but an Occidental, while the preposterous Eli Wheeler solemnly and pontifically explained how the treasured secret of that great "true" trick had been smuggled from the ghettos of Bombay.

"As you see," he said, "the rope is standing straight in the air. To prove its absolute rigidity, that little boy will now climb it. *Look* at him, he is climbing the rope."

When the afficionados broke into applause, Saxon could remain silent no longer.

"Notice," he said, his voice resonant, "the billows of smoke. That's to hide assistants high up on either side of the narrowed stage. One of them catches the rope and secures it to a steel bar."

As if someone had throttled him, Eli Wheeler croaked: "*Who is that?*"

"When the boy reaches the top of the rope," Saxon went on steadily, "he will be out of sight in a cloud of smoke, and one of the assistants will use that moment to snatch him away. Then, presto, as you see there on the screen, the smoke clears, and the boy has 'vanished.' "

The afficionados had turned, glaring at Saxon. Eli Wheeler was off his stool, waving a cane.

"Turn on the lights."

The lights went on, but perversely, the projection machine continued to roll, the silent, black and white images still dancing across the little screen. Wheeler was limping toward Saxon, in such a towering rage that even his vision was evidently distorted.

"*You . . . you,*" he sputtered.

He raised his cane as if to strike down with it, then stopped, his face working, the cane slipping from his fingers, clattering to the floor, afficionados staring at him now, instead of Saxon, their leader somehow seeming to have turned to salt.

"Who is he?" somebody demanded.

Old Eli Wheeler could scarcely get the words out, but when he did it was with reverence.

"It's—Joseph P. Saxon." He kept staring. "*The Great Saxon.*"

The assorted group of afficionados could not believe it.

"I swear, it's *him,*" Eli Wheeler babbled, "him, in person. He is here."

Pandemonium. It was as though Satan himself had appeared before a lower sect of devil worshippers. The men and women gaped, tried to smile, backed slowly away. Then a woman pushed forward, fell to her knees and kissed his hand.

"Get up," Saxon said harshly.

But that only triggered the excitement. An incantation of voices:

"Mr. Saxon, Mr. Saxon—"

"Have you come to perform for us?"

"None of those masters we saw on that screen can equal you."

"You are the true disciple of black magic."

"Surely, Mr. Saxon, you are mystic."

"No magician before you has ever performed *true* magic."

Saxon said: "I have not come to perform for you. I ask that you all go home. I am here to talk to your friend."

He looked at Eli Wheeler, and the clubfoot seemed to squirm inwardly.

"I have to return the film to the exchange, Mr. Saxon, but I'll be right back."

He reached for the projection machine without realizing it was still running. A magician on stage was getting out of a locked box.

"You're not going anywhere," Saxon said.

"No, of course I'm not going anywhere," Wheeler affirmed shakily. "What was I thinking?"

The reel ran out, the spool still turning, film flapping noisily.

"The magic department is open for business," the clubfoot announced.

"Not tonight. I want to talk to you alone."

Eli Wheeler nodded, tiny beads of perspiration spouting like miniature tears on his worn, jaundiced face. "I am flattered."

It took several minutes to clear the store, Saxon sternly refusing to sign autographs, and in the end the afficionados backed out, as if retreating from the beloved, unholy presence of the Dark Prince.

Saxon closed and locked the door, then turned and faced Eli Wheeler, who stood across the long room putting the spool of film into a can.

"I can't imagine what brought you to my humble menage

of cheap, amateur tricks, Mr. Saxon. But whatever the reason, I'm certainly glad you came."

"So am I," Saxon said tartly. "Until here, tonight, I had absolutely no idea what went on in the outer fringes of lunacy."

"You must forgive us, sir. Magic is our world. For most of us, there is nothing else."

"You deceived those people. At least some of them."

"So do you, sir. At least some of them. That's the game, isn't it? Deception."

Saxon resented being put in the category of an operator of a third-rate magic shop. Or was it he didn't want to admit the words had a ring of truth? In a rare fit of controlled temper, he said cruelly:

"Mr. Wheeler, why don't you offer me an exploding cigar?"

Eli Wheeler lowered his head. "To exist I must deal in crude practical jokes. Magic alone isn't enough any more."

Again the clubfoot had stung back.

"Did you enjoy your trip to Las Vegas?"

Wheeler's head came up, his sweaty, aging face blank here in the cold, drafty store. "Las Vegas?" It was a whisper.

Saxon went on: "I imagine you were impressed when Professor Marvelous produced a bowl of live goldfish for his audience."

"He sent for me. I—"

"Then why did you whisper 'Las Vegas' as though it was a place somewhere in the depths of hell you'd never heard of?"

"Because it was a fool's errand, Mr. Saxon. He was very mysterious on the telephone, 'cryptic' might be the word. But when I got there and found it was simply a scheme to promote a magic act for your former assistant—" He shrugged. "What was there to do but spend a day or so and come back?"

"I want to know why the two of you were so interested in Ellen Hayes."

Eli Wheeler busied himself with cleaning up after the afficionados. "For my part there is no interest." He paused, looked at Saxon, his ferret eyes blinking. "Over the years George Dekker has been notorious for his crackpot, get-rich-quick schemes. I should have learned my lesson by now."

As if compelled, Saxon was suddenly looking past Wheeler to a cardboard game box displayed on a shelf.

Eli Wheeler
presents
The Chinese Water Torture Trick

"But they say," Wheeler was continuing, "the older a man gets—"

"Wheeler, are you a manufacturer?"

The cripple looked back over his shoulder at the box.

"No, sir, I leased my patent on that to the Delta Company. It hasn't sold very well. At least, I haven't gotten rich."

"How many other game copyrights do you own?"

"Oh, none. That was it, sir. My one and only."

"Where is Ellen Hayes now?"

"I have no idea. I saw her perform with George Dekker, but I was seated at the bar, it was somewhat noisy, and I couldn't really evaluate her skill. After the show, I met her briefly, and that was the last I saw of her. A lovely, radiant girl, I must admit, however—"

"Where was Dekker's wife all this time?"

"Mr. Saxon, I didn't even know he was married. Must have happened during the past five years because—" He nervously shifted the clubfoot. "I didn't see any wife."

"You slipped in, saw the act and left?"

Wheeler nodded. "After a short talk with George."

"Why would he want to keep you a secret?"

"I'm not aware that he did."

Wheeler was correct: the game was deception, and Saxon's head ached with a shadowy cobweb of answerless questions. Why had Dekker blatantly lied about the attempted liaison with a clubfoot when to admit the truth would have relieved his wife's intense jealousy? To throw Saxon off the track, of course. But what track? Where did it lead? It seemed to Saxon that the murk clouding Ellen's disappearance was no less than sinister.

He looked at Eli Wheeler and knew he'd get no more from him, for a kind of resolute calm had settled over the clubfoot. Anything else he pried out would amount to an endless maze of complicated lies, and since he felt sure this peddler of exploding cigars and toilet-shaped bars of soap no longer knew Ellen's whereabouts it was useless to pursue further. Saxon had reached a cul-de-sac and unless he could think of some possible reason why both this man and George Dekker had been interested in Ellen— Suddenly now, Saxon was talking:

"Wheeler, let me ask you something. The Magnificent Kashi did the slashing-a-woman-in-half with a Damascus sword and created a sensation wherever he performed it. I am sure there were magicians everywhere who wanted to know how it was done. Unfortunately, if the mechanics of an illusion can be penetrated and a rival wizard can imitate, or even improve upon it, the originator has no recourse. But when imitation is impossible the only way to obtain the secret is from the inventor himself. In that case, what would it be worth? What would Kashi's great secret have been worth if he had decided to sell it?"

He looked to Eli Wheeler for an answer, and saw that the clubfoot, in the act of putting aside the high stool, was frozen as if from paralysis, unable even to look back at Saxon: the leering skull, Frankenstein, hideous ogres, grotesque witch masks hangng above his head, and the Chinese Water Torture Trick on the shelf behind him.

The clubfoot's sudden spasm of immobility alone clued the answer.

As Saxon hurriedly left the place, the tiny Santa Claus behind the plate glass window kept bowing at him, as though it, too, was an afficionado.

IN THE state of Florida alone there were twenty-seven department stores that bore the name of Harris, not counting two under construction; the founder of the chain, Artemus, had died several years ago, and his heir, J. T., known to Floridians as "the crown prince," entrusted its entire operation to a Board of Directors that had increased his wealth two-fold, giving J. T. (the J stood for Junior, the T for Timothy) a great deal of free time to follow whatever pursuit or whim took his fancy, which so far had included three wives, an assortment of mistresses, a stable of race horses, summers in the Greek Isles, a large yacht, a priceless collection of paintings, two opera houses that had failed, and the publication of a big, glossy magazine ostensibly devoted to "live entertainment," but actually designed to exploit the "glamour and excitement in the fantasy world of magic." Published every other month at a dollar a copy, it lost money from the beginning and folded after going two million dollars in the red. Rather than reviving public interest in magic, there were those unkind enough to say it had buried that once prevalent form of stage witchcraft.

But J. T. Harris' interest in the fine art of legerdemain never flagged; magic was not just his hobby, it was an obsession. He owned every book on the subject ever published, some four thousand volumes, and it was said he had gone to great expense to obtain famous stage illusions that he himself presented to private audiences. He had been host and invitee to conventions of magicians in every major city. Scarcely a month passed without a telegram from J. T. announcing some soirée or other for "wizards of the wand," which was his name of endearment for professionals.

The playboy department store heir was now in his forties, wore a year-around tan and expensive sports clothes, and had traces of serious good looks; but he was an innocuous sort, and though at times crassly overbearing, had an almost vapid personality. Saxon had met him on numerous occasions but, except for the fact that a man of such enormous wealth creates an aura of self-glamour, hadn't considered him worth cultivating. But then Saxon was not a mixer, was obsessive about his own solitude, and through the years had been disinclined to accept invitations to be J. T.'s guest for a cruise on the yacht, a skiing party in the Swiss Alps, or a vacation on a small island he owned somewhere in the Tahitian group.

But last night after leaving the magic shop it had been imperative to reach him no matter where he was at this particular time of the year. If invisible forces were drawing Ellen into a mystifying net of impossible entanglement, J. T. Harris might be the unwitting force motivating it.

In his room at the Mayfair Hotel in St. Louis, Saxon had made half a dozen calls, and at last located the playboy on Big Turk Island in the Bahamas. After a verbal struggle to get past a snotty male secretary, J. T. came on the phone.

"Joe, this is a real surprise."

Saxon told him it was necessary they have a serious talk.

"I hope you mean in person," J. T. said, then added, to cinch it: "I never discuss anything serious on the telephone."

"Yes, I feel it should be in person."

"Good. How soon may I expect you?"

"First flight out of here."

There was a pause, then J. T. said: "It's a little late tonight. I'll book you a seat on National first thing in the morning."

"No, I'll handle it," Saxon said.

"All right, shoot me a telegram of your arrival time in Miami. I'll have the Lear-Jet waiting at the airport to hop you over here to the island."

"Fine."

And now, aboard the tiny Lear-Jet, streaking across the sparkling, azure water below, Saxon thought of his ordeal in the hotel room last night after hanging up on J. T.

He had pulled a chair to the middle of the room, turned out the lights, and sat in such total concentration of blanking everything out of his mind that it drained him physically. Yet he rigidly maintained the cone of open emptiness, waiting to receive an extrasensory signal from Ellen; next, he zeroed in, thinking of her, visualizing, keeping her in mind's view, the green eyes, that scrubbed, fresh face without makeup; images and flashes that put together the whole woman; that night in the compartment on the train, tawny hair covering half her face, the other half in shadow; a playing card, the three of hearts with a tiny fingernail crease; the girl in the Boston dressing room with tears in her eyes for a dowdy little widow who wanted to "contact" her dead husband; Ellen in his loft apartment, with her pastrami sandwich, as heavy rain poured past the large front window. "Hello . . . Ellen . . . hello . . . Ellen . . ." Calling to her mentally. "Ellen . . . listen . . . where are you?" Diligent as a ticking telegraph key pressing with increasing urgency. "*Ellen* . . ." An hour went by, then another. But there was no communication. Silence echoed with still, cold silence. The ESP was gone. Then, in the third hour, his head aching, muscles taut and screaming, an impression took form. A shadowy figure in unidentifiable darkness. Ellen, asleep in bed. It was there a single instant, then faded like a wisp of vapor. The picture was gone and no amount of mental anguish could focus it in again.

He broke the trance, stood up, snapped on a bed lamp. Had his subconscious tricked him by making a picture he wanted to see? Had the painful weight of tension sought a release and presented illusion, not reality, to break the agony? He fumbled with a cigarette, lighting it with trembling fingers, for a more frightening thought occurred to him. Had he been sure in that flash photo that she was asleep? Or was she dead? Lying there, motionless, dead. No, *no*. It was easier to let himself believe he had imagined the whole thing. ESP is not possible without participation of both parties. Ah, but was he positive of that, either? Had his intense, profound, hours-long vigil been rewarded by transporting his spirit for one single moment to the presence of the "subject?" Had he not, in fact, actually been standing there in that room, wherever it was, looking at her? Hindu mystics had claimed that power for centuries and there had been no evidence to refute it. Attainment. Transference of the entity of Self.

It was only the beginning of a real break-through, but it excited him, left him all but sleepless the rest of the night.

The Lear-Jet dipped its cone-nose, and Saxon saw Big Turk Island beneath them, a patch of tropic green framed by shimmering blue water; and then they were making the approach to the runway.

J. T. Harris was not there to greet him, but he saw him minutes later, at the poolside bar near the hotel the millionaire had taken over for himself and friends. He was clad in slacks, a

striped blue and white T-shirt, and a yacht cap, his face
bronzed, as usual, eyes bright. He climbed off the bar stool and
offered Saxon his hand.

"First time you've ever condescended to visit me."

There was an edge in his voice, rancor, a petulance, and
Saxon knew now the meeting would not go smoothly. Young,
beautiful bikini-clad girls, most of them topless, seemed to
abound everywhere, at the bar, lying around poolside, and in
and out of the water. Only gradually did Saxon notice there
were also men in attendance, and on closer observation saw that
none of them were much under forty, some considerably older:
J. T. obviously protecting himself from competition. Jot that
down in your notes on life, Saxon told himself. A rich man can
people his world as he chooses.

"You know how busy I usually am, J. T."

"Bullshit, buddy," J. T. said, "busy at what—being a ghost
hunter?"

Saxon smiled wryly. "I lead a secluded life."

"Sure, sure, it befits the master of legerdemain to contemplate his navel."

"I was under the impression you were happy I was coming
here."

J. T. grinned. "I am, Joe. Believe me, I really am. On one
condition. I'm giving a show tonight, and if you're in the audience, I forgive all past discourtesies."

"I can't stay that long."

"Oh, no? The island is sealed. Without my plane to take
you out—"

"All right, you son-of-a-bitch, let's get right down to business."

J. T. laughed, and backed up. "Hey, Joe, you really *are* a
sourpuss. I was putting you on."

"You're *not* giving a show tonight?"

"Yes, I am. But if you can't bear to see a really fine amateur magician perform his mystifying feats, I'll ship you out."

"What I came to talk to you about is important."

"Make you a deal," J. T. said. "Come in and look how I've converted the lounge-bar into a theater and instead of making you endure watching me bumble through a magic act, I'll describe the illusions I hope to present. For your approval, or disapproval, and qualified comment." Then, seeing Saxon frown: "Just the highlights, old buddy."

"When do we talk?"

"After that."

"Do you have any idea at all what I'm here to discuss?"

"Not the slightest."

Following J. T. into the lounge-bar, soft music filtering through loudspeakers, Saxon had deep misgivings. J. T. had been overbearing, but Saxon himself had been cross, abrupt. J. T. was, if you analyzed it, a lonely man who, despite all his wealth, had devoted much of himself and his money to an unending crusade to perpetuate magic and the "wizards of the wand." Saxon, as the current top in the field, had ignored him and now, on the playboy's own grounds, had refused to stay tonight and see him perform. God, we're all children, children, Saxon thought, playing our games, and I don't mean to step on anyone, least of all a child like me.

The Turtle Lounge, lavishly decorated with coral, seashells, faded fish nets, turtle shells and pearl, was plush and exciting. A stage at the end of the room that usually featured a trio was where J. T. would perform tonight, and straight chairs had been arranged in rows, facing it.

"My first trick," J. T. said, sounding as professional as possible, "the 'warm-up,' will be to vanish a bird-cage with a live canary in it. I simply open my hands, and presto—"

"The canary is crushed to death."

J. T. smiled. "A facet of your character. You don't believe in murder. Even of birds."

The trick was a portable bird-cage device that was attached to a strong spring behind the magician's back. When he opened his hands, the cage split, the sides of it slamming in under his tailcoat. Instant-out-of-sight, reducing the live canary to feathers.

J. T. climbed up on stage. Saxon remained by the bar. There was no one else in the room.

"All right," J. T. said, "next I present a flower pot, and before their very eyes—"

"—A miniature orange tree grows out of it."

"Joe, you know them all, don't you?"

"I try to."

"So do I try to."

"I've heard."

"Anyway," J. T. went on, "to their utter astonishment, the audience sees leaves sprout, and then real oranges appear on the limbs of the tree."

The "real oranges" were designed from a cloth substance.

"J. T., know how long ago—and when—that trick was invented?"

The playboy scowled. "No, don't tell me. I paid good money for it."

"1796," Saxon said, "by Chevalier Pinetti. A fine wizard of his time."

"I'll be God-damned."

"It was used for a century: air inflating the tube that appears to be a tree trunk, and pressing out the leaves, then the oranges."

"I was taken."

"Don't worry about it. Your audience'll eat it up."

"I sure hope so."

Saxon looked up at him. "Don't you ever *read* any of those books on magic?"

"Who has time to read?"

"Get to the climax of your act."

"Oh, that'll really get you, Joe. I mean, even *you*. Wish I had one of my assistants here to help me perform it. It requires an assistant."

Every man groping through life, Saxon decided here, now, for the first time, needs a warm feminine assistant to help him over the shoals.

"All right, since she isn't here," J. T. said, "I'll describe it. And if you doubt I can bring it off, stay tonight and watch. I appear with a small package—about the size of a cigar box. I announce that my girl is inside. Then I put it down on a low table and the package slowly grows until it's as large as a packing case. I remove the lid and a real live girl steps out."

Saxon softly applauded the unseen illusion described by the T-shirted magician there on stage.

"Got to you. Right?"

"Got to me," Saxon said. "That illusion cost much?"

"Plenty."

J. T. climbed down from the stage, walked over to, and around behind the bar.

"What are you drinking?"

"Scotch," Saxon said, "water back."

J. T. made drinks for them both, then leaned his elbows on the bar, shoving the yachting cap up off his blonde hair.

"What you're saying is, that's one trick you've never heard of."

"Want the truth, J. T.?"

Frowning, deflated, he nodded. "Always."

"Bantier de Kolta. France. 1875."

J. T. looked at him insolently. "And I suppose you think

you're the first magician ghost-breaker. I had it looked up before you got here, and I can name at least four. Maskelyne, Professor Anderson, Kellar and Houdini. They all exposed ghost frauds."

Saxon gazed down at the drink in his hand. "Let's get to what I came here for."

"I guess we haven't anything else to talk about," J. T. said coldly.

"These 'new' stage illusions you pay for."

"You've made me wonder. *Is* there anything new?"

"You know there is. How much have you offered for it?"

J. T. looked straight at him. "I once offered *you* a blank check. All you had to do was fill it in."

"Other than that, what price have you put on the ghost-materializing-of-Lida?"

"You selling?"

"J. T., I'm asking a question. Did you put up a bounty for what is probably the last magic secret in the world?"

J. T. paced from one end of the small bar to the other. "In big business, industrial spying goes on day after day—for 'secrets.'"

"How much did you offer?"

J. T. faced him again. "At the last fête I gave for people interested in magic, which, by the way, *you* didn't attend, I may have, drunk or otherwise, mentioned 'Lida' would be worth a hundred thousand dollars. But why all the concern and agitation, for Christ's sake? Nobody can get the full details except from you, and if you're going to sell, you'll come to me and by playing it cozy probably jack the price up to a quarter of a million or so—knowing my gullibility as you do."

Saxon's voice was cold and flat. "You didn't realize that when you said one hundred thousand dollars, the word would go out, grapevine, and that there are thieves, degenerates and morons who know they could never get the ingredients from me, but *might* from one of my young lady assistants."

J. T. didn't believe it. "I am sure, unless you told her, the assistant has no way of understanding the full procedure."

"But these craven little people who consider themselves 'experts' on magic probably imagine if they get *enough* of it from her, they themselves could supply the rest. Then come to you and put the trick in your lap."

"Joe, half of them think you're super-normal, that it's real black magic."

"I'm talking about the other half."

J. T. studied him. "What are you really trying to say?"

"My last assistant, Ellen Hayes, is in trouble, and you have to be the reason why. That offer."

"Jesus, Joe, I never—"

"No, you 'never,' but you did."

"What do you want me to do?"

"Get word out the offer is cancelled. By telegram. To all of your people connected with magic."

"I'll do it within the hour. Where is this young lady now?"

"I don't know where she is," Saxon said, "and more importantly, *how* she is. I have no idea where to start looking for her. The sad truth is, I don't know much of anything about her. I met her in Chicago, and with your 'permission,' I'm headed there now to find out what I can."

"With my 'permission,'" J. T. said warmly, "and in the Lear-Jet. I'll get clearances at O'Hare. Although I'm sure she's okay." Then, staring at Saxon: "Joe this thing's really got you bugged. Why?"

Saxon put down his empty glass, and admitted to both J. T. and himself something he had just this moment realized.

"I'm in love with her."

XI

"SHE'S IN LOVE with you."

Hushed words in the hush of a dark December day; snow pirouetting past a maze of Christmas decorations, glowing strings of lights and wreaths and golden bells and white reindeer, department store windows shining with gifts, street-corner Santas clapping mittened hands to keep warm. Here in the taxicab, muted strains of a haunting melody, sound of tires slapping wet pavement, the girl beside him on the seat. Sherry. Sherry, bundled up in a furry white jacket, a furry white hood over her head, tucked neatly around the cameo of her pretty face.

Except for the Chicago residence, the discotheque had no previous address for Ellen Hayes, and going to the apartment she had shared with another go-go dancer, Saxon ran into Sherry coming out, headed for work.

"What do you mean, do I know where Ellen is? I'd have sworn if anybody did, it'd be you."

"May I take you to the discotheque? We can talk in the cab."

"Okay."

In the taxi, his first question had been why would Sherry have sworn if anybody knew Ellen's whereabouts it would be him; and that had been her answer, her voice just above a whisper: "She's in love with you." As though it was exactly that simple.

And now Saxon stared straight ahead, over the shoulder of the driver, through the snow-flecked windshield, its wipers sluicing back and forth, traffic ahead, trucks, cars, cabs, people crossing the street; the gay facade of tall buildings, snow falling slowly past.

"But I scarcely knew her before we left Chicago."

It sounded hollow, not enough, and the words hung there, their sound meshing with the thread of sad melody coming through the radio speaker. Sherry looked over at him.

"That's the stupidest thing I ever heard."

"Why?" Saxon was defensive.

"Because you knew her well enough."

"If you're insinuating—"

"I'm not insinuating anything, Mr. Saxon, just that she knew *you* well enough to realize she was in love."

"But I never made so much as a pass at her here in Chicago."

"That came later, huh?"

"There were no endearments, nothing was said about—"

"Does it have to be said?" Sherry too, was now staring straight ahead.

"I'm not a mind-reader."

"Oh, come on, Mr. Saxon, that's one of the things you *are*. I remember Ellen saying: 'He looks at me, and I see myself in his eyes.'" Now she snapped: "You slept with her, didn't you?"

"That doesn't necessarily have anything to do with—"

"To her it did." She gazed at him. "You don't really know her very well, do you?"

He couldn't bring himself to return her look. "If she'd just once said—"

"I guess she was afraid to."

"W*hy?*"

"You're not that dumb, are you?"

"I might be."

"It's obvious. She was waiting for some sign from you."

"And I—didn't make any sign."

"You must be one hell of a cold guy. Real snowman."

"I don't mean to be." He sighed. "If only—"

"Saddest words ever spoken," Sherry said. " 'If only.' *If only* a lot of things it'd be a better life. I have a few 'if onlys' of my own. But I guess nothing compared to the way Ellen must feel. I mean now that you've dumped her."

"I didn't dump her. There was no real—"

"Don't make it worse, Snowman."

"I'm *looking* for her," Saxon said.

"What happened? You have a booking and need an assistant?"

"We don't seem to be getting anywhere."

"*I* don't know where she is," Sherry said.

"Look, we're almost there. Could we stop? Coffee or something? Do you have time?"

She thought about it a moment. "I'll take the time."

A table in the coffee shop of the Sheraton Hotel, snow somersaulting past the plate glass windows. Sherry pushed the hood back to her shoulders, running fingers through burnished dark hair.

"I'm taking the time," she said, "because I want you to know how it really was." She put a cigarette between scarlet lips, and he lit it for her. "Some of you creep men. I don't know what you think we are."

"I wish you weren't so bitter."

Sherry shrugged. "Oh, hell, sometimes I wonder what's the use of anything. Then I'd remember Ellen and say to myself, 'Well, look, she made it.' " She glared. "And now you're here saying she didn't."

"If I can find her—"

Sherry was no longer listening. "I remember that night I came home from work. Bushed. I was really beat. But there was Ellen, happy as a lark. Three in the morning, and she's prancing around, packing her clothes—including that magic act costume of hers, coattail, top hat. You probably saw it."

"No, I didn't see it," Saxon admitted.

Sherry said: "That was the night I knew it was for real with Ellen."

Ellen was wearing tight-fitting black matadors and a green wool sweater, blonde hair hanging past her shoulders. A suitcase lay open on the bed, and because she was exhausted from go-go dancing the whole night through, Sherry was at first provoked. All the bustle of activity probably meant she wouldn't be able to get to bed much before daylight. Ellen sensed her concern.

"Don't worry. I'll have this stuff out of your way in no time."

"Oh, that's all right, honey," Sherry said.

After all, she thought, goodbye to a roommate calls for some kind of crazy little ceremony, and she suddenly realized she was going to miss Ellen Hayes: always bright and cheery, dispelling gloom when it came; and besides that, an excellent housekeeper, whereas Sherry was inclined to be a bit sloppy.

"What time did the magic act ring down tonight?"

"Eleven sharp," Ellen said. "We had a full house, by the way. I was so pleased for Joe. It picked him up. And, Sher, guess what? I was absolutely brazen. I said when we get to Boston, why rent two hotel rooms when one'll be cheaper. He looked at me in a very special, darling way and said he'd think about it."

"Really throwing yourself at him."

"With him I have to. He isn't like any man I've ever known. He's indrawn, like he's brooding over something he's lost, or something he can't find, something he always, always keeps looking for."

"You're hoping you're that something."

Ellen reached for the collapsible top hat, popped it open, and plunked it on her head, but it was reflex action, something-nothing to do. She sat down on the edge of the bed, and as Sherry started shedding her clothes, said solemnly:

"Yes, I *am* that something. Don't ask me how I'm so sure, I just am. Not that *he* knows it yet. But he will. Tomorrow night, in Boston, he'll know."

"Going to tell him you wanted to be a lady magician?"

Ellen took the top hat off, collapsed it and tossed it into the suitcase. "No, probably not because, well, I'll explain it to you, that isn't the point."

Sherry reached into the closet for her terrycloth robe. "All right, baby, what *is* the point?"

Ellen got up from the bed and moved around the small apartment, completely absorbed in what she was saying: "There's an old axiom that somebody probably found in a Chinese fortune cookie or something. 'The electric light went on in my head.' Well, it did, it actually did, and I see things more clearly than I ever have before. *And*—it's wonderful."

Sherry couldn't help but notice the way Ellen's eyes were shining. "You *look* like it's wonderful."

Leisurely crossing back and forth, packing a few more garments, Ellen went on: "People start out in life to do something, or be something, they're usually not sure what; like when I was a little kid, putting on plays with other children, brassy enough to invite adults to watch; then when I was about ten, the magic tricks to amaze and confound the neighborhood brats."

Sherry moved into the bathroom and started removing her makeup, listening as Ellen continued:

"I had it easy, I really did, because I was pretty, 'what a pretty little girl,' they'd say, 'so dainty and cute,' which must have hurt my sister Stella because she never got that much praise. Yet, Stella never complained, I'll say that; she was my biggest booster, still is. But I was the princess of the household. Thinking about it now, those were very good days. What a pity you don't know they are 'good days' until after they're gone."

Ellen came to the bathroom door, watching in the mirror as Sherry labored a comb through her hair.

"In high school, being cheer leader, those were good times, too; then campus queen. I never told you I was campus queen in my senior year, did I?"

"You said you were Miss Louisiana."

"Yes, that was summer of the same year, when I was eighteen. Miss Louisiana in the Miss United States Contest. What a rigamarole, all those preliminary beauty contests leading up to that finale, and I'm such a nut, I'd cry when some of the other girls lost. Going around with the winner's crown on my head, crying for them. Idiot, me. Only they thought I was crying for happy." She paused. "Then, after that, three full years as one of the water ski queens at Cyprus Gardens."

"Must have been great."

Ellen nodded. "But the point is, and I *am* trying to come to the point, there was always something extra in my life, little special goodies, and I just knew I was going somewhere; so finally I started out for the real career, the 'big time' as people used to say, though I'm no longer sure just *when* they used to say it."

Sherry came out of the bathroom now, and Ellen followed her into the bedroom.

"Your 'magic lady' act," Sherry said.

"Yes, off I went, bound and determined, but I couldn't get any bookings; and I thought, I can't go home empty-handed, whatever will people say, after my fine beginnings and all, so I kept going."

Ellen broke off, went to the suitcase, closed and locked it.

"And where did I end up? A gilded cage in a discotheque. In the midst of a chaos of moral disintegration that's sweeping the world. Go-go dancing without a bra. Miss Louisiana in the Miss United States contest on TV from coast to coast."

She walked to the window, pulled aside the curtain.

"But where are *they* going—those people behind all the dark windows; the huddled souls riding an El train at three-thirty in the morning; the street cleaners down there. Everybody, everywhere."

She pushed the shade back in place and faced Sherry.

"You see, I *know* where I'm going. That thing, whatever it is, people keep searching to find, for a woman it doesn't have to be success in a career, or business. For a woman it is much simpler. It can be a man, and for me it's Joe Saxon. He's kind, intelligent, gentle and unbelievably lonely, groping, the way everybody is, but he's something else, too. He's magic. I belong to him, and with him. As I said, he doesn't know it yet, but he will, and when he does I'll be the biggest success in life you ever hope to see."

"There, Snowman," Sherry said, "that's who and what you dumped."

A wind now, flurries of snow darting by the window of the Sheraton Hotel coffee shop.

A Greyhound bus in the pouring rain. Ellen inside, crying hard. The bus pulling out.

"Say something, Mr. Saxon, the least you can do is say something."

Clang, clang, clang, railroad wig-wag. The napkin, the salt shaker. Bam. The napkin flattened. Salt shaker vanished.

"Hey, is something the matter?" Sherry asked.

Ellen on water skis at Cyprus Gardens, spray on either side of her.

"Forgive me," Saxon said, "I wish everybody to forgive me."

Sherry was staring at him. "She *said* you were spooky. She also said that about you."

"And now, coming out on our stage is Miss Louisiana. Lovely Ellen Hayes, age eighteen."

"She's in trouble, Sherry."

"What? Speak up!"

"Ellen's in trouble and I don't know where she is or how to help her."

"Oh, God."

He touched the old building with his magic right hand. Instant vacant lot.

"And it's inadvertently because of me."

He touched the alarm clock and it vanished, the clatter of its ringing receding into darkness.

"What kind of trouble?"

"I don't know. She was in Las Vegas. But she broke her contract. She won't be able to get another job there. I'm sure she left. Is there any chance she'd come back here?"

"No, she hates Chicago."

"Think she'd go home? Where is her home? Louisiana, of course. What city?"

"Baton Rouge. But I don't see her going home," Sherry

said. "There's a guy there she used to write to. Grant something. But after she met you she said if Grant had been the answer to what she was looking for she never would have left."

"Maybe he's the answer now."

"I doubt it." Then Sherry had a sudden inspiration. "She calls home at least once a year. On Christmas Eve. A promise she made her parents. I was with her when she called last year. Her father's name is Charles. Charles Hayes. You could call him Christmas morning and see whether she checked in."

XII

AT FIVE O'CLOCK on Christmas Eve he was in front of a battered, wooden frame house on the outskirts of Baton Rouge. It was a dark day, it had been dark the whole eighty-mile trip from the New Orleans airport where he had rented the car. The flight from Chicago had been bumpy, and with the holiday rush on, the airline ticket almost impossible to obtain. Then the long drive, the sky leaden, and music pouring through the car radio. He must have heard *I'll Be Home For Christmas* at least five times, and because the poignant words made him melancholy, was tempted to turn it off, and yet didn't; didn't because the hope had possessed him that just maybe a forlorn girl in trouble might come home for Christmas, and it was as if by switching off the music he would somehow stop that from happening. Such reasoning didn't make an iota of sense, but it was his mood today. Jingle bells, and ho, ho, ho, have a happy.

The ramshackle house was dark; there were no lights on, and when he rang the doorbell there was no response.

He climbed back in the car, drove downtown, had dinner at a restaurant, and returned an hour or so later. A small, old, beat-up sports car was parked at the curb, and lights were on in at least one room of the house.

He again rang the bell, and after a few moments the door opened and a young man stood looking out at him. A kid, Saxon thought, a college boy, big, strapping, ruggedly handsome, with crew-cut hair, probably belongs to the sports car out front. Though he was impeccably dressed in suit and tie, the clothes seemed alien to him, as if the tie cramped not only his style but some of his breathing.

"Yes, sir, what can I do for you?"

"Is this the residence of Mr. and Mrs. Charles Hayes?"

The boy nodded. "Only thing is, they aren't home right now. Expect them shortly, though, if you want to drop back. Who'll I say called?"

"Name is Saxon. However, they don't know me. Actually, I hoped to get some information about their daughter Ellen."

The young man reacted. "You know Ellen?"

"I did for a while."

"When did you last see her?" He seemed excited.

"It's been something like three weeks."

"Come in, Mr. Saxon. Please come in. I'm Grant Sawyer."

And now Saxon looked at him again. Grant. The name Sherry had mentioned. The man back home. Ellen's sweetheart of a few years ago. But he isn't a "man." Hold on, Saxon, he most certainly *is*. Twenty-three, maybe twenty-four, Ellen's age. Then why does he seem so much younger, less mature than Ellen? Or is it that we look at women differently? A male in his early twenties can be dismissed as callow youth, while a female is ageless. Jot that down, too, Saxon thought, and maybe in time you'll learn to evaluate cause, effect and human complexities. It'll disturb you some, but you have to face up to it.

He was in the house now, gazing in quiet wonder at the large living room. It was quaint and old-fashioned: a Currier &

Ives print of home and hearth in some other era. Huge old lamps, a settee, big, soft, easy chairs with homemade lace doilies on the arms and back, and a footstool on the floor. All that was missing was an old time Victrola. A log was burning in the fireplace, the little tongues of red flame flickering brightly, and close by was a tall Christmas tree, decorated not with clusters of lights, but instead arrays of gum balls wrapped in old tinfoil, little penny red-and-white candy canes that had been placed just so. Long strings of popcorn intertwined the tree, puffs of cotton simulated snow, and assorted Christmas cards played a still game of peek-a-boo between the branches. A heap of gaily wrapped packages nestled lovingly under the lower branches. Grant was closing the front door.

"None of us have heard from her in some time," he said. "Last letter was from Chicago. She works in a bookstore there. Sit down, Mr. Saxon."

Saxon sat tentatively on the edge of the settee, trying to remember whether he had seen any books in that discotheque where he had found Ellen.

Grant Sawyer moved to the fireplace and stood with his back to it. "It's one of the biggest bookstores in the world," he went on. "Has a whole section devoted to magic tricks, parlor games, books on hypnosis, and like that. That's her station, and four times a day she stands behind the counter and performs magic." The young man with the crew cut spoke almost with awe, seeming to envision Ellen exhibiting marvels of sleight-of-hand. "The customers are, of course, attracted and she sells a lot of merchandise that way. Where did *you* meet her, Mr. Saxon?"

"In Chicago." He lit a cigarette. "I was one of those who was attracted. The fact is, I'm a professional magician and after I saw how clever she was I hired her as my assistant."

"My, that must've been a thrill for her. Working with a real for sure magician. She loves magic."

"Yes, she told me."

"Where did you see her last?"

"In San Francisco. My tour of theaters was over, and she was on a bus headed for Las Vegas."

Grant frowned, then brightened. "I suppose they have bookstores in Las Vegas as well as anywhere else."

"Yes, I'm sure they do," Saxon said. "However, I've heard since then that she left Nevada."

"Oh?"

"I've just received new bookings for my act, and since I happened to be in this part of the country," Saxon lied, "I thought I'd drop past and see whether—if anybody here knew where I could find her."

"I sure don't," Grant said, "and that's why I'm here. Her folks expect she'll call tonight on the phone and I thought— well, maybe I'd have a chance to talk to her." He seemed suddenly embarrassed. "I just bet you wonder what I'm doing, barging into the Hayes' house like this, lighting the fire and all. I want it to be warm and comfy when they come home. But, anyway, as I started to explain: they think of me as part of the family." He grinned boyishly. "And the back door never is locked. So—" He shrugged.

"Where do you think Mr. and Mrs. Hayes are?"

"Gee, I couldn't say offhand. Some last minute Christmas shopping most probably. They'll be here."

Saxon gazed at him. "I assume you've known Ellen for a long time."

The boy nodded. "Practically grew up together." His face clouded now. "I used to pull her pigtails. All that kind of thing. Even made fun of her when she had braces on her teeth. Then in high school, the braces off by then, of course—" He seemed terribly anxious to jump to high school. "I played football."

"Bet you were good."

"Ellen used to save my clippings."

"Only a star player gets newspaper coverage," Saxon said, nudging him along.

"That's kind of you to say, Mr. Saxon."

"You must have been 'big man on campus' in that high school."

Grant looked away, enveloped in a rush of nostalgia. He was too modest to admit that he had indeed been big man on campus, but it showed on his face, shone in his eyes. "It was real hunky-dory," he said. "A blast all the way."

"And Ellen was campus queen."

"Oh? You knew?"

"I heard."

Grant pulled at his collar, obviously uncomfortable with the tie around his neck, and now warmed to the subject. "We were going steady during that time, and we were something special."

Special. That was the word Sherry said Ellen had used.

"Must have been the most popular young couple in town."

"That's putting it mildly. Boy, when she was with me, I was Ole King Cotton himself. The city fathers once gave a dinner dance in our honor. That's what it said right on the invitations, in silver engraving, 'In honor of the year's two out-standing teen-agers, Miss Ellen Hayes and Mr. Grant Sawyer.'"

Saxon smiled. "She got first billing."

"Southern chivalry, sir," he said seriously, "the lady must come first." Then he went on excitedly: "That was the night they announced we had been selected to represent the city of Baton Rouge in a Mardi Gras parade up in New Orleans. We were the only ones on that float. Ellen has a picture of it in her room. Would you like to see it?"

"She still has a room here?"

He nodded. "Just like it was when she was going to high school. Nothing at all changed. Preserved completely. Her Mom thinks Ellen may come home again—for good. And that's where she'll stay until the two of us are married. Hey, I'll go fetch that picture."

"Could I see her room?"

"You want to? Sure. Why not? Come on, I don't think her folks'll mind. They're real genial people, Mr. Saxon."

It was a small room, utterly feminine, and the aura of Ellen was everywhere in it; a loveliness time had not dimmed: a period of life and living, hopes and dreams, all were crowded in here; even tears and laughter had their place in the silence. It was something *felt*, the tender sensitivity of it embracing him, as though her arms were around him. Then, suddenly, it was real. It wasn't the past, it was now. "*Joe . . .*" her voice. He started to speak her name aloud, then seeing Grant react to his startled expression, said it mentally, "*Ellen.*"

"*Joe, you're with me. I feel it.*"

"*Ellen, where are you? Where are you?*"

"Mr. Saxon," Grant was saying, "what's wrong?"

And the thread was broken. The presence of her entity, the perfect moment of ESP clicked off. He tried to calm himself, but couldn't, gazing about the room as though it was *he* who had grown up here, the pennants on the wall, *Vassar, Harvard, Yale, Army, Navy, USC,* crazy, non sequitur kid stuff, all of it was familiar. The single bed, the long-legged, flirty-eyed Raggedy Ann doll propped against the pillow; a vanity, a mirror, a scrapbook lying atop the table.

"Mr. Saxon—"

"I'm all right."

"You had the funniest look."

"It's gone now."

"Here. Here's the picture."

Saxon took it, gazing at the glossy eight-by-ten. A float in a Mardi Gras parade. Grant was a kind of Sampson holding up the world, and nestled among cushions on top was Ellen in a gorgeous, flowery gown, waving graciously at people who thronged the side of the street.

"The theme," Grant said, "was 'Today's Youth,' and we won third place." He took the picture back, gazing at it fondly. "We were seventeen that year."

We were seventeen that year . . .

And now Saxon understood why Grant Sawyer was here tonight waiting for Ellen's call. Why, on Christmas Eve, it meant so much for him to hear her voice. It was his wild hope that if Ellen returned they would be "special" again. The golden twosome, and the glory and adulation would be at hand once more, restored, made permanent. Grant closed his eyes to the fact there was another high school football hero this year, and another pretty campus queen. At the age of twenty-three, maybe twenty-four, he was living in the past.

"Grant, what college did you attend?"

The young man put down the picture of the Mardi Gras float. "Daddy always intended me to go to L.S.U., but it didn't work out. He sorta depended on we'd get a 'football scholarship,' as they say. Only I didn't. There are some things that just *don't* work out. So, temporarily anyway, I'm working for the Gulf Oil Company. 'Temporarily,'" he mocked himself. "For the past three and a half years, if you want to know the truth. And it isn't as fancy as I made out. I pump gas and wipe off windshields."

It didn't work out for Ellen, either, Saxon thought. These golden people are now showing traces of tarnish. Isn't Grant Sawyer intelligent enough to realize nothing can ever be the same again?

They returned to the living room, talking of small things, Saxon excited beyond reason at having made actual ESP contact with Ellen. He *hadn't* imagined it. It had been true. He could scarcely bear to listen to Grant Sawyer prattle on emptily. An hour passed. It was obvious even to the young gas station attendant that Saxon was restless.

"I just don't know what happened to Mr. and Mrs. Hayes," he said. Then, frowning, made a guess. "Hey, they might've gone over to her sister Stella's house for Christmas Eve. Stella has a couple of kids, and that'd be kind of Christmasy—" He jumped up, started dialing the telephone. After a moment or two: "Hi, Stella? This is old Grant boy. Is your Daddy and Mom there?" He held his hand over the receiver. "Yeah, they're there." Another wait, then into the telephone: "Hello, Mr. Hayes? I'm over at your house. I thought Ellen might call." A long wait then, dully: "Thanks, Mr. Hayes. Merry Christmas to you too, sir."

He put down the telephone and turned to Saxon.

"Ellen called—"

Thank God she's apparently all right.

"—Probably area code dialed it the first time, but when there was no answer—I guess it was before I got here—had the operator make it person to person, suggesting her sister's number. Not that she wouldn't talk to Stella, but it was her folks she had to reach because—"

"—She'd promised."

"Yeah. Anyway, they talked to her." He was deeply morose.

"Where was she?" Saxon demanded. "What city?"

"They don't know."

He picked up the phone and asked to speak to the local chief operator. Twenty-two harassing minutes later he discovered the call had been from San Francisco. After another eighteen arguing minutes the number from which the call had been made was located.

It was his own.

XIII

SHE HAD FLED Las Vegas, coming to the closest large city, looking for him, seeking haven, comfort; and, he saw now, urgently needing to tell him there were desperate people who wanted to steal his Lida illusion, had threatened, perhaps even physically harmed her in the effort to get it. After what Sherry had told him yesterday in Chicago, he should have realized San Francisco would have been Ellen's immediate destination; but he had been too distraught; aching, guilty sadness clouding his mind, and instead of reasoning it out had rushed here to Baton Rouge, only to talk to a boy she had known once: as though leafing through a musty scrapbook of yesteryear while the vital minutes of now, today, slipped away like quicksilver.

Hands trembling, he was at the telephone again, dialing the San Francisco code area, then his own number. Well, at least now, he thought, the frustration is over, I'll be talking to her, not trying to reach her through a void of ESP. The phone began to ring at the other end of the line, and Saxon smiled over at Grant Sawyer, who wasn't sure what was going on, and beginning to betray by his expression that whatever it was, he didn't like it.

Two rings, three, four, five.

And it finally occurred to Saxon that although Ellen was standing there in his apartment, looking at the instrument as it rang on and on, she thought the call was for him, and out of courtesy would not answer.

He slammed up the receiver, Grant staring at him now as if at a madman.

"Who'd you try to call?"

Saxon took a five dollar bill from his pocket and put it down.

"Right now I'm going to make some calls to Mosiamt and see if I can get a flight out. That should cover the charges on the Hayes' telephone bill."

Mosiamt was the New Orleans International Airport and before the young man could answer, Saxon had put through the first of what was to be a marathon of calls from one airline information desk to another. No, there was no available space on any airliner going anywhere, not tonight, tomorrow, or even the day after. Oh, certainly, he could show up and stand by in case of a last minute cancellation, but there were other standbys already ahead of him, and it was extremely doubtful there would be anything at all.

Saxon put the receiver gently back on its cradle, and looked up at the boy.

"Nice meeting you, Grant."

"Pleased to have met you, sir." A wait, then: "Do you expect to see Ellen?"

"Certainly hope so."

"Wonder if you'd do me a favor. Ask her to call me. She can reverse the charges. It's very important," he went on. "More important than even Mr. and Mrs. Hayes realize."

It was important to an ex-high school football grid star who had stayed too long at the fair.

"I'll tell her."

"Merry Christmas, Mr. Saxon."

"Merry Christmas to you, too, son."

Mosiamt. Skyport dining room. A plate of food in front of him he could scarcely touch. Music filtering through the loudspeaker intermittently giving way to a soft, husky feminine voice announcing arrivals and departures. Outside the window, the airfield flooded with light, big passenger jets roaring by, lifting gracefully into the air, red and green running lights flashing.

Flying away, while he sat by the window seeing the reflection of his desolate face in the glass.

He was on standby with every company flying planes in and out of Mosiamt. He had inquired about a private charter flight, none were available. He tried to get through to J. T. Harris to ask for use of the Lear-Jet, but the millionaire had left the Bahamas and was himself in flight on this Christmas Eve. He and Santa Claus, Saxon thought. He had acquaintances in the city a few miles away: the Chief of Police, and Nick Serano, a Lieutenant of homicide who had also been along at the Sacramento meeting. Yet he did not call them. What could they do? Give him a police escort by car from here to San Francisco? Siren going, red lights flashing over icy, crowded holiday roads?

Returning to the airlines counter, he found crowds queued up at each checkpoint. Roaming the terminal, he watched the arrival gates, saw whole families coming through, being embraced by waiting friends and relatives, faces wet with lovely tears; he observed men, women, children scurry up the departure ramp, turning to wave a goodbye and to blow a kiss as *Jingle Bells* echoed through the loudspeakers, and in all his life he had never felt so alone, so alien.

He walked to the wide, dark window and gazed out, not at

the bustling airfield now, but the sky, blue and alive with stars festively decorating the outer fringes of the infinite: advertising eternity, and he tried ESP again, because that was all that was left, the only link between him and the girl in his apartment in San Francisco. But he couldn't seem to reach her.

The night passed in slow agony, cups of coffee, cigarettes, people milling everywhere—coming, going, waiting. Flickering TV screens all over the terminal. Benches to sit on. Newspapers to read from the first page to the last, even the classified ads, which had never before seemed so fascinating and tragically personal: *Wanted, female. Receptionist, pretty, 25 to 30, dental office.* What pretty young woman would fill that job? Between the age of twenty-five and thirty, wasn't there something better? Where had she wasted so much of her life that there was now only this? *Wanted, male. CPA. References required.* Mister, if you're a CPA how come you don't already have a job? If you had one and foolishly lost it what kind of reference is that going to get from your former employer? You're one sad son-of-a-bitch on this Christmas Eve, aren't you? You, the one who will answer this ad is who I'm talking to. You probably have a wife, kids, and a pile of bills. How *did* you lose that last job? Boozing? Embezzling? Don't you recognize your responsibilities in life? Is a bet on a horse race more important than being a solid citizen? Shame on you. You're weak, is what you are, like all of us. But happy New Year, anyway. *For sale, private party, almost brand-new Ford Mustang.* Dear Mustang owner, you have come to me for my help, and I ask why are you selling that almost brand-new car? A death in the family? Are you a recent widow and now suddenly need money?

Ave Maria coming through the loudspeaker.

He put the paper aside and looked up. My God, *is* she a recent widow?

Ave Maria . . .
Have I become uncanny, a "sensitive" tuned in to human suffering; has my ESP gone out of control, its antenna wires undone and probing, raw ends beckoning to hear in dark corners?
He rose and walked again.
Up tight, I'm up too tight.
I'm imagining every bizarre theory ever offered by crackpots.
"Boy," Ellen had said in that Boston dressing room, "*you* are spooky."
He *felt* spooky.
Super-normal. The word J. T. Harris had used.
I have penetrated the edge of night.
Hell I have. It's this simple: I'm going nuts.
"The greatest perceptive truth is often recognized by the totally insane."
He had read that somewhere.
"*Flight 628, departing for New York is now loading at Gate 12.*"
They were flying in and out all through the night.
God damn it, I'm *not* totally insane.
That's what all the maniacs in padded cells keep shrieking.
"Merry Christmas, Uncle Jim," a young voice yelled happily.
"Honey, I swear—" a different voice, older, "—I'll be back right after New Year's. Oh, Jesus, please stop crying."
Loudspeaker, voices singing: ". . . Little Lord Jesus lay down his sweet head . . ."
Cold, gray dawn had tiptoed up and now pressed mistily outside the huge glass windows.
It was Christmas Day.

I see that your stocking hanging there in the fireplace is chockful of candy, nuts, cookies, oranges and apples. What else did Santa Claus bring you?

No, kids, no opening presents until I've had a sip or two of my coffee.

Ellen, for God's sake, listen to me. Make your mind a blank. Isn't that the way you instructed me that rainy day on the train? Let me get through to you: I'm going to telephone my apartment. This time answer. It'll be me who's calling, so answer.

Concentrating deeply, his eyes closed. "Answer the telephone when it rings."

But she didn't.

It rang and rang at the other end of the line, but no one answered.

At two o'clock Christmas afternoon he found a drunk who possessed an airline ticket to Los Angeles, and when he refused to sell it, dazzled him with sleight-of-hand, adroitly picking the pocket the ticket was in, while at the same time depositing twice the amount of the fare. The drunk was arguing furiously with a uniformed man at the departure gate as Saxon passed through and boarded the plane.

It took off at three-twelve, New Orleans time, and some three hours later set down at Los Angeles International Airport. With the time zone change it was a few minutes after four in that city, and there was now the problem of booking a flight to San Francisco late on Christmas Day. However, shortly after eight P.M., Saxon was off and away, landing in the Bay City an hour later. Then, of course, the long ride from the airport.

At a quarter of ten Christmas night he turned the key in the door of his loft apartment.

But expectancy no longer buoyed his spirit. Midway on the flight from New Orleans he had experienced a sudden deadening let-down, and now as he opened the door a fury of emptiness rushed at him, and he knew without looking or calling her name that she was not to be found in his old, rococo apartment. He would be denied again. It was part of the nightmare that the things he vanished were never seen any more. Yet he came inside and called her name, anyway, and searched the kitchen and bathroom, the gloomy still and utter quiet stifling him. He had seen the tiny Christmas tree at once. It hadn't been important until he was positive Ellen was not here.

Now it was very important, and he walked up to the fireplace where it stood, and knelt on the thick rug, inspecting the little tree, two feet high, a dwarfed replica of the one he had seen in Baton Rouge, strings of popcorn intertwining its meagre branches, puffs of cotton that simulated snow, and several small candy canes daintily sprinkled throughout. There was even a single present lying under the tree, gaily wrapped, and tied with a ribbon fashioned in a bow. It, too, was quite small.

He picked it up, feeling Ellen on contact with the night-blue wrapping, the way a sensitive can read impulses by touching a ring, a key, an old letter. He could see her kneeling here, as he was now, and tenderly placing it under the tree. No "to and from" card. Had she been concerned he might return with that woman he had spoken to her of on the train, and didn't want him to have to answer the embarrassing question of "Who is Ellen?" But what if Marge had walked in and found Ellen herself here? As if reading the answer from a heart print on the tiny package, he realized she must have been prepared to get out the moment the front door opened. But how? The back door, of course, through the kitchen.

He dropped the small present, got up and raced into the kitchen, opened the door and stared down the empty back corridor.

"Ellen!"

He ran through the hall to the rear stairway, his shoes clattering down the cement steps. He stopped on each floor, staring into empty passages dimly lighted by twenty-five-watt bulbs, and called her name, his voice echoing hollowly from the walls, then evaporating in shadowy silence.

He reached the street, looking up and down. Passersby. Strangers here in the chill night. The clang of a cable car. But Ellen was nowhere to be seen.

He returned to his apartment feeling foolish that he had run after her because his extrasensory instinct told him she had actually been gone for several hours. She had perhaps planned a flight if Marge came in, but that had been at an earlier time, and, as it turned out, unnecessary.

He went back to the fireplace, again knelt before the tree and picked up the present, opening it now, carefully so as not to ruin the bow. It was, as the label read, the "Magic Coin Box Trick." This sixty-seven cent "illusion" for sale in all magic shops consists of asking someone to mark a coin he could identify later. You then put it in your pocket and three seconds later produce a box bound by rubber bands. The person who marked the coin is invited to open it, and when he has done so, he now discovers a match box, also tightly secured. Upon opening that, a small red sack is seen, the mouth of it, too, clamped shut. Yet the marked coin is inside.

However, the magic coin box was not new; it, the match box, the little red bag, and even the rubber bands showed signs of wear. Obviously then, it had been part of Ellen's repertoire of magic.

"Thank you."

He said it aloud.

Somebody, after all, had remembered him with a gift.

XIV

THE SHOCK was total. It settled into his pores, it tranquilized his consciousness. If subtle changes had come over Saxon after his return from Boston, specifically, following his days, and yes, the nights, with Ellen—and he had been aware of a mysterious, subliminal force slowly creating an eerie euphoria—the metamorphosis was now complete. Like a snake that has shed its skin, layers of him, too, had peeled away: the crass, the material, the petty. There was now a clarity, a new depth had been attained, though one fraught with murk so that much of it could not be defined, even guessed at; he knew only that it wasn't madness, a power had been bestowed akin to occult; and now instead of scurrying about the country in search of Ellen, who was no closer, and no farther away than ever, it behooved him to remain here, hone the ESP and whatever else, God only knew whatever else, and find her, and making solid communication, talk to her, discover her whereabouts and then go to her. Nothing else was important: for in this time apart had found in her the answer to life.

A man known for his solemnity, he now became a "silent," shutting himself off from the outside world; he answered the telephone only because it might be her, rudely hung up when it wasn't. Never once leaving the apartment, he sent out for food which he seldom ate. His hours were spent cross-legged on the floor in meditation, in awareness, and to him there needed be nothing else, except Ellen.

He had found traces of her everywhere. Specks of his talcum on the floor beside the shower; the imprint of her head on one of his pillows. She had smoothed it out, but if you looked closely, it was there nonetheless. He had deduced without effort that she had initially gained entry through the little area where he set his waste basket to be emptied: double doors, one in the kitchen, the other in the hall. She had obviously crawled through this narrow aperture on hands and knees. There was evidence she had been either tortured, brutally beaten or both before her arrival here: band-aids, gauze bandages, medicines, healing salves—all had been depleted. If her face was battered, she hadn't wanted to be seen. A refuge was needed.

He looks at me, and what I see in his eyes is myself . . .

Why didn't I see it, too? Because I had stopped believing in myself is why I didn't see it.

He knew it had to be Eli Wheeler, perhaps with an assist from Professor Marvelous, who had tortured or beat her, and thinking of that put him at his lowest ebb, the closest to violating his monastic solace. He could fly to St. Louis and confront the clubfoot, but it was also quite possible he would kill him. And since that horror phase was now seemingly over for Ellen, why? He was sure J. T. Harris had sent the telegram that would dispel the greed that motivated the attempt to get the secret of the Lida illusion. Why wreak vengeance for an act in the past when it was only the future that was important? When he was with Ellen again, it would be another matter. The only thing that mattered now was to reach her.

The days passed, and when it was New Year's Eve he didn't know it, or hear it, or care. He sat in darkness and once, for an instant, captured a glimpse of her: a big, blurred closeup of Ellen. It was the saddest face he had ever seen, then it was gone. But he was encouraged. His tuning was close. A bit more twisting of the dials, a lot more patience, and he'd find the true wave-length.

Then, on the third day of the new year, he did.

Better than that, he went to her.

The uncanny feat astonished, wildly excited him. The first clear breakthrough.

In the beginning there was a darkness superseding any he had ever experienced, the astral body gradually emerging; then it was free of the physical, floating, as if to the ceiling, and he looked down and saw himself seated on the floor below, and instead of alarm, felt a serenity: yes, there I am. Calm. Utter calm. And traveled then, as if through a galaxy that diminished time, space. Perfect calm. All at once he was in a city, he didn't know where, standing on a sidewalk. A woman, a small girl, and two men were there with their backs to him, looking up at a plate glass window. He gazed into the window and saw Ellen. She was dressed in the magic outfit, coattails, high hat, long, sheer pantyhose extending from her black shorts, her blonde hair combed smartly to one side of her head. She had a little stand in front of her and was performing card tricks.

Saxon saw her very clearly, the green eyes, pug nose with freckles around it; her clear complexion, the white blouse plumped out by standup breasts; her long, shapely legs, the high-heeled shoes she was wearing. He wanted to go to her, but he was not here physically, was not visible, and though he perhaps spanned a great distance from the living room of his apartment, could not move again, seemed rooted to where he stood. He kept watching her.

"Hi, kid."

But she was not aware of his presence. He had transported his entity without use of telepathy from her end. Why can't I go to her? I want to go just a bit further. I want to be inside that window. Yet he could not budge himself. He looked around for bearings, some clue that would tell him what city he was in, and discovered his vision was limited to the window only, and the casual passersby who paused to watch Ellen's act. He attempted ESP, but she went on, disappearing cards, reaching up and "materializing" them again, unaware. It was as though the window itself screened her, blocked the communication he was striving to achieve.

"Kid, I'm here. Tell me where we are. I have to find you again."

But she was absorbed in her work and there was no response. He continued looking at her, sick with the longing he felt; and sick with himself for abandoning her on that dismal, rainy day in San Francisco. What was it Sherry had called him? "Snowman?" No feelings. God knows that isn't true. I submerged the emotions that tore at me, and that are assailing me now.

Without realizing how, he sensed his time here was up. He rebelled against departure, but though he had been awarded a gift that bordered on black magic itself, he could not will his astral being to remain. Then, in the fleeting moments left, he saw the child and her mother. The little girl was pointing up at Ellen.

"Look, Mommy," she said, "the magic lady is crying."

And he, too, saw the shiny glisten in those green eyes, and in his voyage away from there thought: perhaps in some strange way, she *was* aware of me; felt the presence of love, and wanted desperately to reach through a void and embrace it.

Earthbound again. Feeling a loss of the fragmentary freedom. His apartment.

But he had been able to go to her, no matter how brief the visit.

Then frustration beset him once more. He had been on a trip without knowing where. Not even the name of the store had been in sight, nor what it was: department store, a Woolworth's, a big toy and game shop. Ellen had been a window display. A live mannequin to attract the public, the job perhaps temporary. He had been within five feet of her, and yet no closer than he was now. No closer, no wiser.

On the tenth of the month, bills came in, as usual, with the rest of the mail. Saxon sorted through them, cast them aside; then, suddenly, was attracted to the bill from the telephone company. Ellen had placed a long distance call to Baton Rouge. Perhaps there had been others. He tore open the envelope, saw his guess confirmed. Las Vegas. A fairly long conversation as the bill was higher than for an ordinary business call. The number was there on the bill, and Saxon called at once.

"John Turk Agency," a woman answered.

"This is Joe Saxon. I want to speak to Mr. Turk."

"I'm sorry, I'm afraid Mr. Turk is—"

"It's urgent," Saxon said sharply.

There was a short delay, then Turk was on the line. "Yeah, Saxon, what can I do for you?"

"You had a call from Ellen Hayes about three weeks ago."

"I get calls all the time from all kinds of broads."

"Tell me about this one."

There was a pause, then Turk said: "Yeah, it *was* sorta interesting, at that. She called a couple of days before Christmas . . ."

Ellen, two days before Christmas, alone here in Saxon's apartment, standing by the table, holding the telephone.

"Mr. Turk, I realize I walked out on the contract I signed at Rainbow's End, but it was just a standard form, and I thought maybe you could take care of it for me and get me back on."

"Babe, way I hear it, somebody took care of *you*. Pretty good."

She tensed up. "How did you find out?"

"That truck driver you hitched a ride with."

"I didn't hitch a ride, he stopped."

"He said you were walking along the road across the desert in the dead of night with your suitcase, one of your high heels busted. In other words, you were limping."

"He was kind enough to give me a ride to San Francisco."

"He described you as all messed up," Turk went on. "I mean he said your face was beaten to a pulp."

"Just when and where did he say this?"

"Las Vegas–San Francisco. That's his regular run. I know the guy, and when he got back here he looked me up and told me."

"Well, I'm all right now," Ellen said into the telephone. "What marks are left I can cover with makeup."

"You remember telling him who used you for a punching bag?"

"No, I don't. I was crying. Hysterical. I probably just babbled."

"A gink that calls himself 'Professor Marvelous,' is one of the things you babbled, and I went over and fixed him for you."

"You did *what*?"

"Found him in that fleabitten casino, Golden Mirage, and kicked the bejesus out of him."

"You shouldn't have done that."

"Maybe not, but I don't like punks that beat up women. Lady, it was quite a scene, I tell you. That little, bitty wife of his, Dana, or whatever her name is, kept jumping on my back and biting me. But I kicked the living crap out of him anyway.

And I'll tell you just one more thing. Everybody in Las Vegas knows about it, and he'll never work this town again long as he lives."

"I suppose you feel I should thank you, but—"

"Yeah, go ahead. Why don't you thank me?"

"What about my job back at Rainbow's End?"

Two days before Christmas.

Was that before or after she had gone out to some street corner and spent what was probably close to the last money she had to buy him the little Christmas tree?

Saxon, on the phone now, still talking to Turk.

"What'd you tell her?"

"No chance of getting her job back at Rainbow's End or any other casino here."

"What'd she say? What was she going to do?"

"Hell, how do I know?"

"Where do you think she went?"

"Probably back to Louisiana. That's where she lives, isn't it?"

It wasn't until after the phone was hung up that Saxon realized the booking agent had made a slip.

Turk had no way in the world of knowing Ellen was from Louisiana.

Looking at the number on the telephone bill, he called Baton Rouge. Charles Hayes answered. Saxon explained who he was and said he was anxious to find Ellen.

"Well, she hasn't come home yet, Mr. Saxon," Hayes said, "but she's a whole lot closer to us. Called little over a week ago and said she has a job at Och's Department Store in New Orleans. She works in a show window doing her splendid and mystifying magic tricks."

XV

THE SAME AREA of sidewalk, the same plate glass window, but the magic lady was no longer inside; instead, there were mannequins, clad in bikinis, mounted on water skis, holding an imaginary tow-line, smiling waxen smiles, a wind machine blowing back the hair of their flaxen wigs; and, as before, passersby stopped between him and the window to look, to gawk, fleetingly, while Perry Cole, a tall, prissy vice president in charge of display for Och's Department Store explained:

"I can't imagine how she got the impression the job would be permanent. It was, after all, simply a novelty. An experiment with a live performer, much in the way—well, once, to advertise a special on hosiery, I conceived the idea of an attractive young lady in a swing wearing our super sheer silk stockings and swinging back and forth there in the window. I *do* strive for what one might call a unique creativity in—"

"In other words, what you're trying to say is, Ellen Hayes was disappointed when you told her the job was ended."

"Yes." Then he hurried on: "As you may already know,

ours are the most talked-of window displays in New Orleans. People just never know what we'll come up with next, and they go out of their way to—"

"Did she say whether she had any future plans?"

"As a matter of fact, merchandising executives the country over come here to—"

"Did she say what she was going to do?"

He looked blank. Then: "Oh. The girl in the window."

"Yes, the girl in the window," Saxon said.

The tall, frail man picked at a blemish on his face. "Come to think of it she was—" He grew angry, "—quite bitter. Which brings me back to the point. I did *not* promise it would be a steady job."

"Bitter how? Explain."

"She was very snippy. That's all I seem to recall."

"Recall a little better," Saxon urged. "What did she say?"

"Something to the effect that she had come a long way for the position."

"How'd you happen to hire her in the first place?"

"She was recommended by our personnel manager. She had been up to see him and he—I believe he remembered her as a former Miss Louisiana. And when I heard of her talent at card tricks and other little demonstrations of magic, I found an immediate place for her. I pride myself that when a challenge is put before me—"

"She mention anything about going home?"

"No, she didn't. What she *did* say was, she supposed she could always get a job as a striptease queen on Bourbon Street. She was piqued, of course. I am sure a former Miss Louisiana wouldn't—"

"Once a queen, always a queen."

"I beg your pardon?"

Saxon looked at the mannequins in the window. "One way or another," he said softly, "the lady has been a queen most of her life."

In his room at the Royal Orleans, he put in a call to Baton Rouge.

"Please forgive me for disturbing you, Mr. Hayes, but I happen to be in New Orleans now, and I thought if you had any idea where I might find Ellen—"

No, Charles Hayes had no notion where his daughter was staying.

"I'll probably be here for the next few days, and if you hear anything at all—"

"Mr. Saxon, is something wrong?"

"Oh, no, sir." His tone must have alarmed Hayes. "It's just that—" he groped, "—she's such an excellent assistant—" Saxon's connotation of "assistant" was not what his voice conveyed.

"Oh, of course," Hayes said, "if I hear from her, I'll see to it she calls you."

And after it was dark, Saxon started a lonely prowl up Bourbon Street, a terrible dread ravaging his innards. Please let me find her. The brief time since that day in December when he last saw her seemed a stone age away. He had known in advance, in some tormented way, she would no longer be in the department store window. All of his other efforts to find her had been thwarted, why should today be different? I'll find her tonight. Yeah, and to the tune of A *Pretty Girl*, while she disrobes, one item at a time. Do they allow completely topless in New Orleans, or must the girl wear pasties?

"Come on, come on, see the sex kittens wiggle."

A sidewalk barker in front of a striptease bar, a checkered suit, straw hat cocked over one eye, a cane, looking like a caricature in a silent movie.

"Real live dollies," he went on lewdly, "stripping down for action."

Saxon went in. The place was small, dark, gloomy; a seedy-looking couple were seated in a booth, and three men were at a table; the bar was empty, and on a miniature stage above it, a skinny, wilted-looking young woman was strutting in high heels, two steps one way, two the other, in time with music being played not by a band, but a phonograph backstage. The record was scratchy, but the song was haunting and beautiful, desecrated now, profaned in this atmosphere, the stripper removing a skirt, tossing it into the wings, strutting, spangled tights, her brassiere next to go. Yes, they wore pasties in New Orleans.

Saxon ordered a drink. Silence, moments of silence, the girl standing up there, waiting, listless until the record was changed. Then, as the music started again, raucous this time, she was animated, standing directly above Saxon doing bumps and grinds, that spangle-encased pelvis, bump, bump, bump, Saxon looking elsewhere, at his drink when the bartender put it down, then at his fingernails, the stripper squealing, as if in orgasm, running fingers through her hair. Bump, bump, bump. Squealing.

Bourbon Street. Barkers and pitchmen, whores and pimps and junkies and pickpockets and con men and car thieves and tourists; the wail of a trumpet; bright lights, flashing signs, second floor balconies, women calling down, cooing "You there, mister," and when that failed to entice, obscenities.

Bumps and grinds, dollie faces, scarlet lips, writhing torsos, "*Take it off, take it off!*" layer after layer of blue cigarette smoke shimmering in mid-air; booze, everybody has booze. The music loud, louder, LOUDER.

"No, sir, there's no exotic dancer here by the name of Ellen Hayes."

I need help. I can't be everywhere. I can't see all of them.

"Nope, she ain't here. Hey, maybe your friend's a hooker. Ask a cab driver. They know 'em all."

Walking, the hard sidewalk. The cold January night. The lights. The noises. Music. Laughter. A second floor window, the shades drawn.

A hooker in a cheap hotel room, lying on her back in a rumpled bed, naked.

No.

Don't ask a cab driver, ask a cop.

Telephone booth. A coin. "Give me police headquarters." Then: "Lieutenant Nick Serano, please. Homicide." Homicide and missing persons worked out of the same division. Now: "I'm a friend of his. I wonder if you'd be kind enough to give me his number at home."

After thoroughly identifying himself, mentioning the New Orleans police chief's name, and describing the meeting in Sacramento, Saxon got the number.

"Joe," Nick said, "I tried to reach you today."

"You did?"

"Yeah, called your number in San Francisco. No answer."

Panic seized him. "Why? What were you calling about?" That sounded too stark. "Business or social?"

"Business. We've got a problem." By "we" Nick meant the police. "Real headache, if you want to know. Hey, what are you doing here in town?"

"What—what is it that's so serious?"

"What else? Your specialty. Somebody's trying to convince us we have a very annoying ghost in the city."

"Oh." Vast relief. "Is that all?"

"Don't think you won't be paid," Nick said. "The city's agreed to come up with a fee of one thousand bucks. More, if you insist. That is, if the gimmickry is complicated. Listen, how about meeting me at my office in half an hour? I was just getting ready for bed, but this is something that shouldn't wait."

"I also have something to discuss with you that shouldn't wait."

"Well, fine, we'll form a mutual aid society."

Nick Serano's office was a cubbyhole adjoining the garage in the basement of police headquarters. It was bare, unadorned, with a cement floor and no windows. There were two desks cluttered with papers, three large filing cabinets, and a tin coffee pot.

"Isn't much," Nick said, "but do you realize there are damned few police lieutenants in the country who have their own private offices?"

Saxon smiled. "No wonder crime runs rampant in the streets."

Nick Serano was a small, husky man of about forty, with a shock of black hair, dark eyes, and a dead-serious face. He was intense, a human dynamo, and yet an affable sort interested in everything. There was no way you could dislike him. The police chief had remarked that even cynical criminals he had put behind bars had nothing bad to say about Nick Serano. He did his job, no more, no less, but he did it well.

He and Saxon had arrived in the basement garage at almost the same time and now, here in the office, Nick plugged in the coffee pot.

"All right, whose problems first? Yours or mine?"

"I hope mine," Saxon said.

It was almost exactly midnight, and within thirty minutes an All Points Bulletin was out on Ellen Hayes.

"Since she's not a 'wanted,' " Nick explained, "this is hardly prescribed procedure. But as long as you insist she may be in some kind of jeopardy I might be able to justify it. If I have to. I doubt I'll have to."

Saxon doubted it, too. Nick was held in high regard by his superiors.

"Anyway," the detective went on, "it means that every

police officer in the city is looking for her. When she's picked up, I'll deliver her to your hotel. In person."

"I can't ask for more than that."

"*Now* may we get to the problem the city of New Orleans is faced with?"

Saxon poured himself a second cup of coffee. "Of course."

"First I'll fill you in a little on the place itself."

Saxon had stated in the Sacramento lecture that a history of the "haunted" real estate almost always explained the reason for what was going on. Ruling out the possibility of a prankster perpetrating a fiendish practical joke, the motive had to be one of immediate or eventual profit.

"It's a rundown motel complex that dead-ends at the river," Nick said. "What with fog and mist coming in off the Mississippi, it's spooky enough as it is. Owned by an ex-con, a slippery little character by the name of George Harms—a junkie, and what-else-have-you, there used to be some pretty wild goings-on. Usually late at night. We raided the place three times and in each instance came up with quantities of heroin. However, nothing we could pin on Harms. There were arrests, but he was always in the clear. I knew he was guilty—was probably pushing the stuff—and it made me sore. As you can gather, I was giving narcotics an assist. I told Harms next time we found even one gram of 'H' on his premises, or any other serious irregularity, his ass was in a sling. Scared the crap out of him because he knew I could make it stick. I'd have him inside-looking-out for the rest of his natural life. So, anyway, the boys in narcotics tell me there hasn't been the slightest hint of a rumble out there in over a year."

"And now?"

"A 'ghost' in Room 104." He flushed. "What I mean, of course, is a contraption that simulates ghostly noises, even a change of atmosphere in the room itself. We've torn the place up and put it back together again looking for bugs, gimmicks, devices—even had the bomb squad out there with sensitive detectors. Nothing."

"How long has it been going on?"

"No more than four days, and the place is empty. Isn't a single tenant that didn't move out. Of course most of them were transients anyway. Now we've got the place closed up."

"Is there a recurring pattern to the noises?"

"Yeah. Once every twenty-four hours, at three minutes after two A.M. You can hear it for half a block, and we get calls somebody is being murdered. In fact, we now post a squad car there at that hour so the public'll see the police are on the scene to take care of things. But we don't know what to take care of. So far, we've managed to keep it out of the papers. They get so many calls from wild-eyed citizens who want to report a ghost or a flying saucer or something they just file it and forget it. Good thing, too, because this one would get front page space, to say nothing of some pretty scary TV coverage, both national and local. We don't want that kind of thing here, so yesterday an emergency session of the City Council appropriated money for your good, and I hope, speedy services."

At twenty minutes before two o'clock in the morning, the dingy, two-story Starlight Motel was shrouded in a swirling gray mist; it stood there at the dead-end in darkness, not a light on anywhere. A police squad car was already parked at the curb as Nick Serano drove up with Saxon.

"I'll wait for you."

"You're not coming?"

Nick shook his head. "I've been there. Joe, I don't believe in the supernatural any more than you do, but whatever's in Room 104, it's God-awful. Frankly, because we *don't* know what it is, it scares hell out of me. It apparently scared George Harms even worse. Of course, he was a physical wreck to begin with, heart condition, a few other things."

The detective stared straight ahead through the windshield

at the swirling columns of fog slithering like coils around the front of the old motel. "Way it was," he went on, "the first night nobody reported all that screaming. If it was a murder, and we of course know," he added hastily, "that it isn't—that would have been the night it happened. George Harms was in Room 104 the second night. Police got a frantic call from a disturbed tenant about the noise. When they arrived there wasn't a sound. Just a huddle of people in night clothes pointing at the door of 104. The officers went in, place was empty, just a vacant room. And George Harms was lying on the floor, dead." He saw Saxon react. "Natural causes. Coronary."

"You didn't tell me he was dead."

"Something else I didn't tell you." Nick Serano was tense now, on edge, still staring straight ahead. "Thought I'd save it for the last. Lab found blood on the carpet. Somebody had washed it off, or thought he did, but it showed up under a microscope."

Saxon said: "I think you're trying to scare me. That could be an old bloodstain from any number of causes."

"No, it was recent." Nick's voice was just above a whisper. He handed Saxon the key to Room 104. "There's a chair by the bed. Go in there and sit down and wait. I think it's best you're sitting down."

"Nick," Saxon said, "you're taking this awfully seriously. There's an explanation, there always is."

"Okay. That's what you're here for. To explain it to us."

Saxon flipped the key up, caught it, opened the door and got out.

He walked through the fine mist of fog toward the cold, dark motel, then along the walk to Room 104. He unlocked it, opened the door, reached in, turned on the light and entered.

He looked around. Nothing out of the ordinary. Clean enough, neat, though old-looking, the blue wallpaper torn in places, the beige carpet worn and spotted. There was a dresser, a double bed, chair, lamp, table and a small TV set. Everything was standard. A bathroom adjoined, the door open. Saxon closed the outside door and looked at his watch.

One minute of two.

He saw the chair by the bed, walked over to it and sat down.

The room was well lighted from overhead, but he also snapped on the bed lamp. There was no heat, and the air was icy.

Saxon gazed about, already trying to analyze the possibility of electronic or whatever other devices that could be cleverly employed to spook the room once each twenty-four hours. There were two small front windows, the shades drawn. Yet a high frequency ray might penetrate such a flimsy barrier. He was thinking it out, asking himself how *he* would go about creating the frightening illusion.

Then it began, the subtle change in atmosphere. The air that was icy with sharp, biting cold now became clammy, there was an odor of musk, it was overwhelming; then, startlingly, a high, ghastly whining began, whirling in a cone, the sound moving here, there, growing more intense, *whining*. Saxon was clutching the arms of the chair. The hideous whine gave way to a sound of breathing that grew and grew until it was as though you could hear a human heartbeat. Saxon's eyes roamed the lighted room. He tried to calculate how such delicate, real sound could be reproduced artificially. Now: someone crying. A woman crying, sobbing, beginning to wail, then, a wild, jarring, terrifying scream that lifted Saxon half out of the chair. Despite his conviction a genuine unexplained haunt did not exist, he was shaking violently.

Suddenly a woman's voice cried out, "No . . . NO . . ." There was the thrashing noise of a tragic struggle, another loud, piercing scream, and still another, long, shrill, reverberating from the walls. Then something touched Saxon. Invisible hands on his shoulders, on the sides of his face, and he was up out of the chair, not simply in terror, but with sudden, terrible, horrifying knowledge, and he himself began to scream, agonized; he bellowed, turned around and around yelling at the top of his voice.

"No, oh, God, no! Oh, no, no!"

Then sank back in the chair, no longer able to stand, scarcely able to breathe.

What he had heard here in Room 104, what had touched him, was the anguished ghost of Ellen Hayes.

 XVI

HE WAS still seated in the chair, face drained white, as Nick Serano rushed in, the two prowl car officers right behind him, guns drawn. The unearthly noises had died away; the atmosphere was a chilly normal again. She was gone. Saxon looked up at the detective, but couldn't speak. He had yet to comprehend that which he knew: a beyond *did* exist. But the profound discovery was blurred, spoiled, meaningless in the knowledge that Ellen was dead. The shock was so great he did not at first hear what Nick was saying, the pressure on his system, the throbbing in his head only gradually freeing him to listen, adjust to the mundane, the earthly human reality: that concert of voices, guilt, recriminations, sex, hope. Hope?

". . . heard you yelling."

"Yes."

The cops had searched the closet and bathroom, and now holstered their guns.

"You can go," Nick told them.

They filed out, and the detective looked again at Saxon.

"You look as if—" he broke off. "I won't say the obvious."

"I didn't *see* her, if that's what you mean," Saxon said. "But yes, there was a ghost."

Nick studied him a moment longer. "I'm not surprised."

Saxon looked up. "Said you didn't believe in the supernatural."

"I didn't want you to to think I was a damn fool. And I never did. Until this business."

He put a cigarette in Saxon's mouth and lit it for him.

"Thanks."

The detective sat down on the edge of the bed, his face solemn, creased. "I was sure a modern police force like ours could flush out a hoax if that's what it was." He himself lit a cigarette. "God damn, cold as a witch's tit in here." He caught himself. "Why'd I use that word? Witch." He looked over. "Where do we go from here?"

Saxon rose slowly, wondering whether his legs would hold him.

"You can start by cancelling that A.P.B. on Ellen Hayes."

That startled the homicide man. "What?"

"It's her."

Nick snuffed out his fresh-lit cigarette. "How could you tell?"

"You've been here when it was happening. She ever touch you?"

"God no. I think if I'd been touched by anything I'd have died." He got up from the bed. "All right, something touched you, but—"

"I know it's her."

"*How?*"

"How the hell do *I* know how? It's her." He turned away. He was crying. "I didn't mean to yell."

"She meant a lot to you."

His back turned, Saxon nodded. "More than anybody ever has."

Nick Serano circled around, looking at him. "Said *you* didn't believe in the supernatural. Was that a lot of crap? Man of your experience prowling through haunted houses must have known the truth."

"I didn't, though. There's so much I didn't know. I thought lately I had progressed in certain dark areas, in fact I did, however all on an earthly sphere. But there's another dimension out there."

"Maybe we'd better go back to the office, have some more coffee, and kick this thing around."

"No," Saxon said, "if you want these two o'clock in the morning sounds to stop, we have to start moving."

For the first time, the homicide cop seemed skeptical. "Has the one man anti-ghost squad suddenly become an expert on the real thing?"

"I've read everything there is on the subject."

Nick Serano shrugged. "All right, what do you suggest?"

"That you start acting like what you are. A cop. Ellen was murdered. There was no body?"

"The only body we found in this room was that of George Harms—and that had to be a good twenty-four hours *after* the murder."

"Then let's have a morgue check—unidentified bodies of young women picked up in the last few days." As the detective nodded, Saxon went on: "One of the things she wants is to be found. Right now she's in torment. She won't rest until something is done. She's been defiled, degraded, her life was crushed out. Nick, that's what she's raging against. And once we can—"

He broke off, because only then did it occur to him if they were able to restore some mark of dignity to her death Ellen might slip away to a far beyond and then be totally lost to him: even if only as a scream in the night.

And yet possibly not. If a super-ESP had kept her earthbound these past few days wasn't there a chance that by seance or some other means Saxon might still somehow be able to communicate with her? Since a supernatural world and beings in it *did* exist, if anyone could bridge it, wouldn't it be someone like him?

No, that's selfishness, born of the loss I feel. I'm already into darkness beyond my depth.

Don't expect any more miracles.

But then do we ever *stop* expecting them?

"Maybe once we can—what?" Nick Serano asked.

They were moving out of the room into billows of cold, wet fog.

"It's not enough that we simply find her body," Saxon decided.

"It certainly isn't for me. It's my job to nail whoever it is that killed her."

Saxon suddenly stopped, looking at him. A shrill, lonely boat horn echoed from the river. "How come you haven't already identified Ellen Hayes? Who was Room 104 registered to?"

"Nobody for the past month," Nick said. "What do you take us for? We checked those registration cards back for over a year."

"Nick, you must trust my intuition. She was living in that room."

"Nobody was living in it. It was empty."

"Did you ask the other tenants?"

"People who lived in this crumb-dumb place didn't talk much. But one of them did say he saw a young woman come and go from 104."

"There you are."

"He's a wino. I didn't believe him."

"What's your notion about finding George Harms lying dead in there?"

"His own room was one door down—the motel office. He heard the screaming that second night, rushed in and died of fright." Saxon started to move, but Nick caught his arm. "If she was living there, what happened to her things?" Before he could answer, Nick went on: "I know. You're going to say somebody moved them. Maybe so. Only *why?*" Again, the detective prevented Saxon from speaking. "Never mind. Give me time. I'll answer those questions myself."

There were only the two of them there in the dimly lighted morgue. A long, steel drawer was pulled out, the nude body of a young woman lying inside, a tag attached to one toe. Her face was battered beyond recognition. Nick thought she was a pretty good bet.

"Found in an alley, just like you see her."

Saxon shook his head. "It isn't Ellen."

"How can you be so positive?"

Saxon's voice was firm, patient. "I know it isn't her."

Nick Serano gave the drawer a shove. It slid back and clanged shut.

"*You* are spooky."

"I've heard that before," Saxon said, "now I hope it's true."

Back in his cubbyhole basement office, Nick said: "Give this a whirl. The guy who killed her—don't ask me how I know it's a man, I'm a little spooky myself—waited till things quieted down, then gathered up her body, took it out and put it in the trunk of his car, went back in, got all her stuff, and carted that to the car. After which he drove somewhere, dumped her body and her personal belongings." He sensed that Saxon wasn't impressed. "What's the matter with that? For starters?"

"Why wasn't she registered?"

"You're the one who said she lived there."

"I still say it. And I think you're partially right about what happened. With one difference. The night of the actual murder, George Harms heard screaming, but if he's a junkie maybe he was high, anyway he didn't respond. But the next morning he remembered, knocked on the door of 104 to see whether she was all right. When she didn't answer, he used his pass-key and went in. She wasn't there, but he saw signs of a struggle, the blood on the carpet, and it didn't take much for him to figure she'd been killed. He was in a panic."

"You mean because I'd warned him if there was another rumble out there—"

"Exactly, you'd throw the book at him. Way he saw it, he couldn't risk calling the police. Particularly without a body. You people'd shake down the whole motel, maybe come up with another batch of heroin or something. Whether it was his H or not, to quote you, his ass was in a sling. And murder on top of that—Anyway, it was Harms who packed up her clothes— probably weighted them down and gave them the deep six in the river—then came back, tried washing away the blood on the carpet, and tore up the registration card. That way it'd appear there hadn't been anybody in 104 for over a month."

"You're probably right. George Harms was just kook enough to do that."

Saxon continued: "The next night when he heard the screams again, he thought she must have come back. To say the least, he was confused. He rushed over, went in and seeing nothing, but hearing those screams, dropped with a coronary."

"You make a damn good detective," Nick said.

"But I believe you're right it was the murderer who disposed of the body. I doubt he'd've chanced waiting around to move her things."

"Try this one: why didn't he just leave her there?"

"Maybe like a lot of people, he believes no corpus delicti, no chance for a murder conviction. And if he's from out of town, which he probably is, thought without a body you'd never be able to tie him up with anybody who had seen the two of them together."

Nick got up from the wooden chair, stretched. "Okay. The next step is what?"

"Find the body. It's urgent. For her sake."

They looked at one another. It seemed odd language. Find a body for the sake of the one who had possessed it. But Nick knew it was true.

Saxon looked at his wrist watch. "It's twenty of four. We should leave now."

"Where do we look first?"

"That's up to you, Nick, you know this town. Put yourself in the boots of the murderer. He doesn't want to go far with a body in the car. So he'll drive along maybe back roads, looking for a swamp or a marsh where with any luck at all the body won't be found until summer. I suggest we return to the Starlight Motel and start from there, same way he did. Let your instinct guide you."

"You don't want to put the entire force on this yet?"

"No, unless I'm wrong, I—I think if we get anywhere even close to the vicinity I'll know, sense it somehow."

He was too embarrassed to explain it further, and Nick didn't ask it of him. All he said was:

"Joe, you're a remarkable man."

"I respect you, too," Saxon said.

The Starlight Motel stood in the cold pre-dawn like a once doomed fortress long since abandoned: darkly morose, the slate-covered river behind it, its foreyard ghostly, empty, and Nick Serano and Saxon, having returned, started from there again, Nick behind the wheel of the car, windshield wipers sluicing away beads of mist that clung to the glass like specks of icy sweat. They were silent, and Nick drove as though the steering wheel was magnetized, making a turn here, another two miles farther along the road. Saxon saw him reach to his pocket for a cigarette, and then change his mind, putting his hand back on the steering mechanism, peering ahead through lacy petti-coats of fog, passing beneath trees whose umbrellas of Spanish moss whispered across the top. When Nick made a third, seem-ing involuntary turn, Saxon saw that he was visibly disturbed.

"I don't know what the hell I'm doing," Nick said. "I've lost all sense of direction. The car is—"

He broke off. He didn't want to say out loud the car was driving itself. He already felt spooked, and to admit it would confound the lunacy. He was, after all, a detective of homicide, a realist who dealt with earthly things: passions that drove peo-ple to murder, greed that motivated them to rob and kill. He'd had a glimpse of the supernatural in Room 104 and he would prefer to limit what he knew of the beyond to that one confined area. He did not want to believe it also existed here in this morbid gray darkness. Or, particularly, that something unseen was guiding the direction of the car. Saxon read his thoughts: simplistic ESP coming through loudly, generated by Nick Ser-ano's secret inner fear.

And now as the car hummed over the wet road, past old houses, across deserted intersections where signal lights flashed yellowly on and off, Saxon questioned his ability to understand so clearly each of Nick Serano's thoughts; but more than that, his own calm acceptance that Nick was not propelling the car in any direction of his own choosing. Could he be only imagining he knew the feelings of the man who sat next to him? Was his interpretation of the car's independent action an hallucination of his depressed mind? Where was truth? Where did reality end and the other world begin? He felt enmeshed in a swirling cobweb of unreality into which he alone had been invited.

"You're just following your instincts, Nick," Saxon said.

"You're a good cop. You know the criminal mind. If the direction you're going seems odd, it's simply that your subconscious has taken over."

Or, Saxon thought, that he's found a beam tuned to the frantic, frightened ESP the murderer left behind like a quivering vapor trail on these lonely back roads. And that at least is earthly realism. A camera using infrared lighting can photograph a parking lot three hours after it has been vacated and the ghost images of all the cars that had been there will be visible on the developed film: an aura left behind created by the energy of their former existence at the site. An aura of thought engendered in a thrashing, terrified mind can also cling in the atmosphere. Saxon was convinced nothing a human being urgently said or did ever really vanished.

"I hope you're right," Nick said, "but let me tell you something. I tried to make a turn at that crossroads back there, and I couldn't." He looked over. "Now don't give me that crap about my subconscious. My subconscious never drove a car in its life. If you want to know, I'd just as soon let you drive."

"No," Saxon said sharply, "keep going."

Streaks of daylight were gouging the sky, he saw a rickety wooden bridge ahead that spanned a steaming marsh, and it was now Saxon who was possessed, held as if by a closed fist. The spirit dominating Nick Serano had transferred to him, and it *was* the unseen, he realized, not a vapor of guilt left by a killer on the night of the murder. Witness: tension easing from Nick —again reaching for a cigarette, this time putting it in his mouth and lighting it.

"Must be losing my cool," the detective said. "I would have sworn—"

The car was clattering over the wooden bridge, and they could hear the hiss of gases from the fetid marsh below. Nick was grim once more, not saying what it was he would have sworn. Then the bridge was behind, the black, open mouth of tree-lined woods engulfing them.

They had traveled less than another quarter of a mile when Saxon said:

"Here. Stop here."

The car skidded, then pulled over to the soft shoulder of the road.

Nick tossed his cigarette out, looking ahead, then behind. "Better leave the lights on. Road's fairly narrow, and if we pull over any farther we'll bog down. Wouldn't want some barreling-assed bastard to ram us from the rear."

They climbed from the car, leaving its head- and taillights glowing. Saxon plunged into the thicket of woods, Nick close behind him, and after a few steps they were slogging ankle-deep through green mire. Saxon turned, looked back at the detective, whose face was now without expression. Impelled, Saxon started off again, presently wading knee-deep, and hearing the splash of water behind him, knew that Nick was keeping up.

Then Saxon stopped again, standing very still; Nick reached him, a question in his eyes, and now both of them heard the low, distant, unearthly whine, as if of a tortured wind lost in the marsh. The swirling, twisting sound of high, shrill whining.

"Oh Jesus," Nick said, out of breath suddenly, "I'm not sure I can take this."

"You wait here."

"No."

Saxon started in the direction of the noise, Nick plodding, splashing behind him, bilious gases smarting in their nostrils, the whining growing louder like a screaming dervish, gas fumes spewing up multicolored handkerchiefs of wavering light; and then Saxon began to run, wallowing in bilge, wading, and Nick Serano remained behind, but could see Saxon flail at the water, the stark spears of pussywillow, the green scum floating on the surface.

The whining became intense. It encircled Saxon as though he stood waist-deep in the eye of a hurricane. Daylight clawed holes in the dark sky. Then he saw a hand protruding from the water and hurrying to the spot lifted the dead body of Ellen Hayes, green slime tangled in her blonde hair, one side of her face eaten away by flat, white parasites that still clung to the bony skull. Saxon pulled the corpse into his arms, hugging it, holding it, moaning. He was in a trance deeper than any he had ever experienced: as though invisible hands were drawing him to the brink of eternity.

Nick Serano, watching it all, was not revolted at the sight of Saxon holding that leech-eaten skull to his own face but was struck with almost instant paralysis by the fact that the whining had stopped and the only sound here in the back bay swamp was the hiss of gases.

XVII

"YOU STOOD THERE holding the corpse, didn't move at all, and I was in a kind of stupor myself at the sudden silence," Nick Serano said. "Then when I finally reached you, you just stood there, hanging onto her, and wouldn't budge. My God, it was cold. The water was icy, and yet you weren't even shivering. If you'd been unconscious you'd have toppled over, so I don't know what kind of a state you were in except you didn't seem to hear me, even though I was yelling my head off, so finally I went back to the car and called for an ambulance. It took all three of us, two ambulance attendants and myself, to drag you in. You were unconscious then, all right, you conked right out on the stretcher, and we went back and got her body; it was already decomposing and part of it—"

"Never mind," Saxon said.

It was past seven in the evening, and he was in a small, private room at the city hospital.

"What happened to you on the way back scared me absolutely pee-less," Nick went on. "You stopped breathing." He paused, fumbling for a cigarette. "The intern was right there with you, and he looked up at me, dumbfounded, and said, 'He's dead.' But then he started massaging your heart, and gave you oxygen, and you finally began to stir, so you couldn't have been dead, young Doc was wrong about that."

No, he wasn't wrong, I remember now. I crossed over. It's all very hazy, but I know for certain I was on the other side, and I was holding her, and she was Ellen again, not a ravaged corpse; she was whole and real and warm, crying for happy, but then she always did cry easily, and she kept telling me something. What was it? I can't seem to remember. She kept repeating it. It was the only thing at all she said. Yet I can't bring back the words. But I was there, all right, in the beyond, and there were dark blobs howling around us, grotesque faces with no bodies, raging and frothing, an inferno of lunatic faces with gaping sockets instead of eyes, while Ellen kept saying those words that now elude me.

Saxon had awakened only minutes ago to find Nick sitting there by the bed, looking at him, and now Nick lit the cigarette he had fumbled with and handed it over. Saxon took it, then cranked the bed up to a sitting position, feeling a mysterious power he had never before possessed, combined somehow with the secret knowledge that he had been on the other side.

There were dark lines under Nick's eyes, and he seemed thoroughly exhausted.

"Looks as if you haven't had much sleep."

"Haven't," Nick said, "none at all. It's been a rather busy day."

"You make a habit of lighting other people's cigarettes?" Saxon asked. "You did that last night in Room 104."

"Only when I think a man needs a cigarette."

"It's very gracious of you," Saxon said, "few people are

that considerate." He surveyed the hospital room now, inspected the wrap-around smock they had put on him. "Sorry people had to go to the bother of undressing me."

"Your clothes were a mess—wet and stinking from that brackish water, and so were mine. I had one of my boys go to your hotel room and get a change."

He rose, opened a closet door. A fresh suit, shirt, tie and even shoes were inside.

Before Saxon could thank him, Nick continued: "You were checked over by the medicos. Said you were probably in shock that you'd likely be all right when you came to."

"Yes, I'm all right."

"Well, they'll examine you again before you can leave here, so count on it."

Saxon looked straight at the detective and asked in a low voice: "Is she in the morgue?"

"No, her father came after the body. He's taking it to Baton Rouge. The train pulls out—" He looked at his watch, "right about now. Funeral'll be day after tomorrow, closed coffin. News media picked it up, of course. The fact that she was murdered," he added quickly, "absolutely nothing about the occurrences in Room 104."

"Big headlines, I suppose."

Nick nodded. "A former Miss Louisiana found murdered? You bet. TV, radio, complete coverage. However, I didn't mention to any of the reporters that it was you who found the body. Not even to her father, for that matter."

"Appreciate that."

"Only protecting myself," Nick said. "They'd dig it up that you're a world-famous psychic detective and there'd be more questions than I'd care to handle."

"I assume you've started a murder investigation."

"Hell of a lot better than that. I have a suspect in custody."

Saxon stared at him. "Who?"

Nick sat down. "Real juicy for the newsboys. A department store executive. Name's Perry Cole. Well known locally for his window displays."

"Why would *he* want to kill her?"

"Mr. Cole has very exotic tastes."

"Spell out what you mean by exotic tastes."

"Among other things, likes a woman to strip down except for a little pair of boots and lay a whip to his quivering backside."

"I don't see any possible connection between that and Ellen, and if the publicity implies she ever participated in anything like that, she wouldn't—"

"*She* wouldn't like it?"

"Neither would her family."

"You said *she* wouldn't like it." The homicide detective was on his feet again.

"All right, she won't."

"God damn it, Joe, she's dead and gone."

"Dead," Saxon said, "not gone."

"You said once the body was found—"

"There's the hell she went through. Not from the murderer alone, but others who, indirectly, in one way or another, contributed to her death."

"You saying that screaming will go on in Room 104?"

"No, I don't think so. But she's still earthbound."

"How in the living hell do *you* know that?"

"Next, you'll insist there's no such thing as a supernatural."

"I admit there *is* a supernatural, but what you're telling me is that you've got it turned on. You claim to be a medium now," he said sarcastically, "with a 'spirit guide' in the beyond and all that other claptrap?"

"What are we arguing about?"

"That deviate I booked for murder this afternoon."

"How can you believe Ellen was one of his girls?"

"I don't, but he was after her. Isn't every woman that can satisfy his fetish, and when he finds one he thinks can, he loses all sense of balance, caution. We've had him up on sex charges half a dozen times in the past ten years. Anyway, Ellen Hayes worked for him—"

"I know that."

"He laid it on the line. If she wanted to keep that job in the showcase window—"

"So she quit."

Nick nodded. "But he didn't. He was observed haranguing her on the street; and he was seen in the parking lot of the Starlight Motel the night of the murder."

"That hardly proves he killed her."

Nick Serano's weary face was white now. "I'll prove it before I'm through. Tell you why. There was a murder something like this one year and half ago. Unsolved. I could never hang it on him—he's a smooth article—but I know damn well it was him, and I'm not going to let a monster like that walk the streets of New Orleans."

"I think you have the wrong man."

"*I* don't, and this is my game, not yours. Far as I'm concerned, we were out of the ghost business as of dawn this morning. Nevertheless, since you brought it up, I want the names of those people you say indirectly contributed to her death."

"They aren't in the city."

"I don't give a shit where they are."

"You wouldn't be able to bring charges against them."

"I suppose *you* intend to go after them?"

"If I can get evidence enough to convict even one of them of physical assault, I'll turn it over to the police."

"You're a real friend," Nick said bitterly.

"Okay. I'll give you the names before I leave New Orleans, but only on your promise to lay off until I can confront them with a certain matter that concerns me personally."

Nick Serano's whole expression changed. "*You're* involved in this?"

"Wasn't I here in town looking for her?"

"Jesus, that's something I completely forgot. *You* might even be a murder suspect."

"Sure, that's why I asked you to find her."

"Could have been a very clever red herring to throw suspicion elsewhere. And who but the murderer would know where the body was?"

"Will you quit talking like a cop?"

"*How* are you involved?"

"The people I told you about were after a very intricate blueprint to a stage illusion of mine. There was a price offered for it—a high price. They thought they could get the basic mechanics of it from Ellen, and for that reason she's been in trouble and on the run for the past several weeks. That's why I think you arrested the wrong man."

"No, I have a hunch about Perry Cole. I think he's our boy. But you go ahead and take care of what you have to, and if you decide one of *them* is the murderer, holler for me."

"Nick, I sure as hell will."

A nurse came in with a pitcher of water. Nick now seemed even more exhausted than before. He ran his hand down over his face, gazed at the nurse.

"Honey, I think this man wants to get out of here. Get a sawbones to come in and have a look at him."

"Yes, sir."

When she was gone, Saxon said: "Nick, go home and get some sleep."

"What about Room 104?"

"I'll go there tonight. Instruct the squad car officers to expect me."

"Fine. Will do."

It was almost ten P.M. before Saxon arrived back at the Royal Orleans. He took the elevator to the twelfth floor, went directly to his room, shaved, showered, put on a robe, then called room service, ordering a dinner to be sent up.

He had just finished the meal when the eleven o'clock news came on TV. He left the cluttered table, walked to the divan and sat down to watch.

A grim-faced newscaster looking straight out from the small color screen: "Ladies and gentlemen, acting on a mysterious tip from an anonymous caller, police early this morning discovered the body of former Louisiana beauty queen Ellen Hayes in swampland twenty miles east of New Orleans. Before noon today a coroner's verdict indicated she had met with foul play. Specifically, she was murdered. Late this afternoon, in a highly dramatic turn of events, police picked up—"

Now on the screen: Nick Serano and another detective escorting tall, unhappy-looking Perry Cole down a corridor in police headquarters.

"—Och Department Store executive Perry Cole as a prime suspect in the slaying—"

A scene on the stone steps in front of the police building, a burly, hatless man with curly iron-gray hair stating that the charge against his client was absurd.

"Police, for some reason, have been hounding Mr. Cole over a period of years."

After a commercial, the TV news continued with an "in

depth" report. First on the suspect: film clips of former Och Department Store window displays. Then suddenly Saxon was staring at the window in which Ellen had appeared wearing the top hat and coattails. There was even coverage on that, and he thought he saw the back of a familiar figure among spectators peering in the window, but the scene ended so quickly he could not be sure, and the news story, with running commentary over picture, now segued into Ellen's appearance at the state-wide beauty pageant where she had been crowned Miss Louisiana.

Her face suddenly filled the screen. Soft, lovely, blonde hair down about her shoulders, tears in the green eyes as she adjusted the glittering crown on her head, trying to smile, but too filled with emotion to manage it. Sound accompanied the film of that long-ago July, the orchestra playing music of regal triumph, applause echoing in the hall; and then Ellen was making her walk along the runway, still trying to smile, tears spilling over, the music swelling. "I was eighteen that year," she had told Sherry. Yes, Saxon thought, yes, you were eighteen that year.

And now, from behind him, hands touched his shoulders.

He jumped from the divan and turned around, but the room was empty, and the soft caress he had felt was gone.

What was it she told me while those lunatic faces howled around us?

Why can't I remember?

I was there, holding her, and I heard the words very distinctly, but now they, too, are gone.

He entered the chilly atmosphere of Room 104 at the Starlight Motel a few minutes before two A.M. Turning on the lights to get his bearings, he shut them off again, walked to the chair by the bed and sat down in the dark.

The fact he was a little early for the usual timed occurrences made no difference. She manifested herself by voice almost at once. A low, hushed, sad voice, and he had to strain to catch the words.

"Make . . . things . . . right . . . and . . . I . . . will . . . be . . . with . . . you . . . always." Then in a rush, like a gently blowing wind: "Please make things right. Please—"

It ended there.

He waited in the damp cold of the room for an hour. There was no other sound.

But he knew they had been the words he had heard during those precious moments he lay dead in the ambulance but alive and aware in the beyond.

"Make things right . . ."

He was stunned. Make things right. Did she mean after that he would be dead and then they would be together always? It didn't matter. He no longer had any fear of dying. But he suspected that had *not* been her meaning, and if it hadn't, what was she trying to say? That she would come back? In spirit, if not in body? Yes, that would be fine, too.

There was so much to comprehend he despaired of any attempt to try and calculate that vast and staggering enormity, yet at the same time was overcome with the realization he had achieved true communication with her. He was positive that with intense concentration he could do it again. And it didn't have to be here in 104. Hadn't she come to his room at the Royal Orleans and gently put her hands on his shoulders?

He decided to return there at once and reach out into darkness.

XVIII

NOW AT four o'cock in the morning the darkness in Room 1240 at the Royal Orleans Hotel was empty. Saxon sat very still in the straight chair he had placed facing the closed portals of the French windows: night and the things of night swirling outside in eerie silence. His concentration was absolute, the doors of his mind, his entity, his very soul, flung open, vulnerable, a slowly revolving antenna, but it seemed singularly alone in a soundless void. Going deeper into a trauma of trance, the emptiness louder in its awful, oblivious silence, he was alone in the universe, forsaken, an invisible speck in an awesome, endless sky that reached to forever but didn't stop there; and tumbling through that skein of powdery blue mist it was as though he would never stop falling; and it wasn't until now he knew that he was in space, and there was no such thing as time, or space either, only galaxies of the infinite, and then, as if to prove it, as though a guide in the beyond had placed him there, he was somewhere else, at another time. It was not his astral body, he was whole, alive.

That drafty dressing room in the basement of the theater

in Boston. A lady in her forties, clad in a shabby cloth coat wet with shreds of icy snow. She is staring at Ellen, believing her to be the materialization of a ghost, and I am saying: "There is no such thing as a supernatural. I've spent my life looking for evidence of the hereafter, but it isn't there. The dead are dead and forever dead."

And then he was tumbling again, arms and legs askew, those absurd words ringing hollowly, mocking, distorting like a phonograph record going at too high a speed, and receding into a void; and he himself suddenly motionless, not falling any more, looking at Ellen, standing the distance of a small abyss from him, a trace of a smile on her lips. "Spirit guide and all that claptrap?" Nick Serano had said. She had led him backward in time. Now he tried to speak to her, but couldn't. He mouthed voiceless words, remembering once in his apartment he had said to *her* there was no such thing as time, and she had answered: "There is at the bus terminal."

Swiftly catapulting back:

The Greyhound terminal, rain pouring outside, Ellen wearing a matching set: glistening white raincoat, hat and galoshes. I am waiting as she stands at the window buying a one-way ticket out of my life. Now she returns to me, her scrubbed face looking innocent and young under that shiny white rain hat.

"The Las Vegas bus doesn't leave until five," she says, *"but don't you worry. I'll buy a magazine to read and wait here."*

A piercing scream tore him from that moment in time.

Room 104. He wasn't there but it was projected in the darkness, a blur of white dots making it impossible to discern the figures of Ellen and the man who is facing her, her voice now calling out: "No, NO . . ."; the thrashing noise of a tragic struggle, the white flurry of dots a blizzard, another loud, shrill scream.

Silence.

He sat there in the straight chair in Room 1240 at the Royal Orleans.

While manipulating time she had lost control and slipped back to the night of the murder.

Now she was gone.

He shook off the trance, started to rise from the chair when suddenly as though by a gust of wind, the French windows blew open, and a misty white figure floated in, coming straight at him, an angry *whining* accompanying the aura. Saxon was back in the chair, flailing out at the wraith, but it moved around and around him like a spinning top, and he was transfixed with horror.

And that was just the beginning, for now it was indeed as though he had succeeded in opening a Pandora's box of black, fetid mysteries, the atmosphere teeming with grotesque imp faces, eyeless loons, all howling, darting at him, circling the room like ghastly phosphorous balloons on which a madman had painted faces, the wraith still coiling around him, breathing now—a loud, labored breathing.

Saxon at last managed to rise up out of the chair but it seemed he had lost his senses, and what he was seeing and hearing was a chimera of the mind; he had delved into darkness and when he pulled his head out his brain was scrambled; it was *he* who was the loon, being stung to death by vipers of his imagination, unable to cope with them, turning about, seeing grinning blobs everywhere.

He yelled at the Things here in the noisy darkness, ran at them, moved drunkenly, half sobbing; he stumbled, fell, got up again, but they were after him, tearing at him. Like swarms of yellow killer bees they flew at him, howling, howling. He wanted to peer into the hereafter? He wanted to visit the unknown? Well, he had pried open the door of the beyond and here they were: ghouls and imps and bloated-faced insects.

Then he saw what they were doing. They were urging him

toward the window. They wanted him to go out that open window and into the vapor of naked night. He resisted, but his strength was gone, his arms and legs crumbling with palsy. He felt the cold air coming through the window envelop him, then as the Things all closed in, beating a wild din in his ears, the last fibre of nerve snapped and he ran for the window, jumped up onto the sill, teetering there, seeing the twelve stories below.

Invisible hands from the outside pushed him back off that ledge, into the room again, and he fell on the bed, sitting there, incapable of thought, then noticed the imps had gone, and where there had been one wraith there were now two misty shrouded images, clashing, the whining sound like the wail of a siren, but gradually subsiding, and when it was over, there was only one wraith, the one that had forced him back into the room.

Saxon watched in dumb shock as it, too, vanished; but the French windows swung closed, the latch fell into place, and he knew it was still here, and that it was Ellen, and though he heard no sound he felt as if she were scolding him; and sitting there, drained, he nodded, chastised, feeling like a small boy, because what she had asked him to do was make things right, meaning: make things right here on earth that had affected her life and propelled her death; but instead, ever the sorcerer, the incurably inquisitive wizard, he had tried to probe the unknown, stir a stick around in that bubbling cauldron to see what would come out, and *had* seen, and heard what, if his sanity was still intact, he never wanted to see or hear again.

The black terror that had erupted through his system like geysers of bleeding vomit began to ebb; his heartbeat was gradually returning to normal, and the prickly fear that had stiffened his spine and crawled up to his neck and even to the top of his head eased slowly away, and all this time he felt her presence; she was waiting, and he tried to tune his mind to her, but his thoughts were still scattered, quivering and disjointed, like a dish that has shattered, and it would take a minute or two, maybe longer to dispel the demons that had corrupted his being.

He thought, fleetingly, with irony, of Chesterfield, Indiana, where each summer for the past seventy years fifty thousand people poured in to what the brochure described as "the hub of world spiritualism," to be victimized by frauds, charlatans, "mediums" conducting group seance, asking inane questions of the visiting "spirits," "How's the weather over there?" the talking trumpets hanging from invisible wires; mentalists performing "eyeless vision" and "pencil reading;" poorly manipulated illusions of levitation; and of course apports—objects from the "beyond" that are ejected from the medium's mouth onto a table: a brooch, a button, a penny.

Suppose just once at a well-attended seance in that spiritualistic convention called Camp Chesterfield there was an invasion of the howling imps; what if a crooked medium in the midst of "materializing" a "ghost" manufactured out of regurgitating cheesecloth splashed with luminous paint, suddenly found herself confronted with the real thing? Saxon had witnessed the alleged professionals at Camp Chesterfield and observed the afficionados of that spirit mania, exposing the fraud in magazine articles; yet the believers still flocked there. There was so much of the unknown that was abused and phony it was no wonder it had been so difficult for him to at last penetrate Truth.

The ripple of a whisper: *"Concentrate."*

It snapped him from the numb reverie. He got up from the bed, feeling his strength restored, and as if propelled, moved back to the straight-backed chair facing the French windows and sat down, seeing now that a tarnish of gray daylight had magically "vanished" the darkness outside. He stared straight ahead at empty air, evoking the power of his mind to see that which was not there, and then, staring, saw the start of what was almost a duplicate of his Lida illusion.

White dots outlining the shape of a woman demonstrated Ellen had begun an ectoplasmic materialization. He watched auric emanations flash from her psychic body: vortices of energy. Chakras, as the Hindus called it. He reached up his arms because he knew the ectoplasm must come from his body—that slightly alkaline detritus and sputum that was his own and must flow into her: his energy combining and locking with hers to give her substance. And little by little, by dint of great effort, she slowly appeared, ghostly at first, then whole, perfect and except that she was stark naked, *exactly* the Lida illusion. However, it wasn't illusion any more, it was reality.

He got up from the chair to go to her, but she backed away.

"No, don't touch me," her voice still only a hushed whisper, "the transformation isn't complete." He stopped, gazing at her, and she went on: "If you touched me I'd disintegrate, and that wouldn't be nice, would it?"

"Do you want something to cover yourself?"

"If I'm embarrassing you."

"I want to look just at you and not think of that."

"All right, darling, get me something."

"Is the substance holding you together too fragile to support the weight of one of my shirts?"

"No, I don't think so."

He stepped to the closet, grabbed a shirt from the shelf, shook it out, and threw it to her.

"It's fine seeing you, Ellen. It's a miracle."

"Joe, it'll be a true miracle when you've made things right."

She seemed obsessed with that phrase.

"I'll do it," he said, "I promise."

She had the shirt on now. It was much too big and she looked pixie-ish standing there.

"When you do, I'll return," she whispered, "and that's when it'll be complete. I'll be a woman, capable of anything a woman can do." She seemed to laugh. "Yes, Joe, anything."

"But how could that be possible?"

"Darling, don't ask questions. You've asked too many already, and it's very dangerous for you. You were almost killed because you went too far. Just take my word that it's possible. I'll have to go back now and then for a few hours; I'll still be a ghost, in that sense, but I'll be with you when you want me. *Do you want me?*"

"Of *course* I want you. Ellen, I'm so sorry for all you've gone through. It's my fault."

"No," the soft whisper said, "nobody's fault. Now hush about it. Certain subjects are not permitted. Until you've made things right I won't be able to see you any more, or communicate. Though I'll help when I can, *if* I can. But don't expect to reach me yourself. And if you can't make things right, I'll never see you again. Even in eternity."

"I *will* make things right. I *will* see you."

"I'll need clothes."

"I'll have a closet full of them for you in San Francisco."

"Undies, too."

"Yes, transparent undies, with lace."

"But no bras. I never wear a bra."

"I noticed."

Ellen in his shirttails, blonde hair down her back, standing barefooted in shadow beside the windows. He was afraid she'd fade away too soon, and went on warmly:

"You showed me proof that old axiom of mine: there's no such thing as time is true."

"It was a prank," she whispered, "but it backfired into a

nightmare. There are nightmares in the other world just as there are in yours."

"Yes," he said, "after what I saw here in this room awhile ago, I can well imagine."

"I'm sorry, darling."

"It seemed a ghost entity of somebody was after me."

"Hush now."

"It whirled around and around the chair."

"Joe—don't talk about it."

"*Your* nightmare was being projected back to the time of the murder in Room 104. It was all hazy—but I saw a man there with you. Was it the image of someone still alive? Yes, I'm sure it was. If I knew his identity, I could make things right in a hurry."

And in his naive assumption the matter could be resolved that simply, he was almost unaware as she vanished and the shirt dropped in a heap on the floor.

He walked over and picked it up, then gazed out the window and saw the silhouette of gray, unwashed buildings in the early daylight; and realized the magic was gone, and she was gone.

For now, at least.

At a quarter of one in the afternoon, he woke with a start, the telephone ringing almost off the hook. He leaned up in bed, answered. A Mr. Nick Serano was in the lobby.

"Send him up."

Saxon left the door ajar, and was in his robe and slippers, ordering a pot of coffee sent up, when Nick came in.

"Get some sleep?"

"Enough." Then Nick came right to the point. "Got something to tell you. It's so weird I don't know what to make of it. Perry Cole was not Ellen Hayes' last employer." He paced the room. "She was hired for one night by Florida millionaire J. T.

Harris to be a magician's assistant." He turned, looked at Saxon. "So happens it was the night of the murder."

Saxon could scarcely believe it. "He's the one who offered a high price for my stage illusion."

"*That* I had figured," the homicide cop said. "Everybody in the country knows Harris is a nut on magic. Used to publish a big, glossy magazine in the praise and worship of 'legerdemain.' Anyway, the thing he gave here was billed as a convention of magic."

"He uses that word once a month," Saxon said, "sometimes more."

"Well, the thing is, whatever he used to do before, the guy has now flipped. Hired a hall, brought in all the props and performed what he called 'an evening of magic' to an empty house."

Saxon felt such genuine alarm it was as though Ellen were still alive, and in danger.

"Obviously staged the whole thing to get close to her," he told Nick. "Ingratiate himself. Prove he, too, was a magician, so he'd have a chance to talk to her, maybe buy whatever details she knew of the Lida illusion."

Nick Serano could not believe that. It, in fact, agitated him. "He could've just walked up to her somewhere and had his little talk. He didn't have to go through all that."

"He's used to paying for the privilege of talking to people."

He was thinking of Big Turk Island in the Bahamas. All the young girls in bikinis, all the male guests, every one of them almost forty or better; and all the "conventions" where J. T. Harris paid the bills in order to assure his popularity; and extended cruises on the yacht shared with a selected list of moochers and hangers-on. Perhaps it had begun to gall him and in a freakish mood he had played to an empty house rather than to an audience of martini-ridden mechanical robots who had seen it all before and would applaud on cue. But then, Saxon thought, who really knows the answers to anybody?

"Ask me," the detective said, "he's one hell of a hot murder suspect."

"You already have a suspect."

"Yeah. It never rains, it pours. Because in spite of that smart-assed lawyer sitting right there beside him, I think Mr. Perry Cole is going to crack. Of course he's such a delicate son-of-a-bitch he might cop out just to get us off his back, then recant at the trial. I've had that happen, let me tell you. And as for J. T. Harris—he's a V.I.P. with a lot of influence in Florida where I have no jurisdiction. Which means: no balls to back up putting out a hook for him. Besides, that isn't even where he is. The bastard has this hotel he's taken over in the Bahamas—British Territory. So he isn't even in the country."

"What you're saying is, you want me to check him out."

"Hell, I'm not saying it, I'm insisting. And if it looks like he's it, don't tip your hand, just go back to Miami and call me. He has to return sometime and I'll put in for extradition papers."

Make things right . . .

Nick was staring, and Saxon asked: "What are you looking at?"

"You. Trying to read your thoughts."

"I'll leave on the first flight for Miami," Saxon said, "and head right over to Big Turk Island. I should be there about five this afternoon."

XIX

THE HOTEL and its facilities, which included a marina, swimming pool, small golf course, the outdoor bar, cottages, and the Turtle Lounge, were located at the far end of the island and looking down from the helicopter Saxon had rented for the hop from Miami he was astonished to see the whole area deserted.

Though it wasn't five in the afternoon there were no people down there, the gay, holiday structures surrounded on three sides by sparkling blue water looking from high in the air like a condemned playground. It had been confirmed the island was J. T. Harris' present whereabouts, but now Saxon wondered whether, acting on some whim of the moment, the millionaire had pulled out, taking his menage of pleasure-seekers with him. Then it occurred to him the reason might be more sinister. Had he heard Saxon was on the way and fled to avoid a confrontation? If so, why drag his retinue along? Or had he abandoned them, too, at some earlier date? Had the hall in New Orleans on the night he gave his magic show been empty because he had at last officially forsaken his own personal flock of free-loading afficionados?

The 'copter hovered over the golf course, setting down on the grass. Saxon and the pilot alighted while the blade was still spinning.

"You wait here," Saxon said. "I'll see if there's anybody around. If there isn't, we'll be headed right back."

He started briskly in the direction of the hotel, and had gone about a hundred yards when he heard his name being called.

"Saxon."

He stopped, looked around.

"This is your wizard speaking."

There was a system of loudspeakers set up on the grounds, and the voice was coming from several directions.

Though he had no idea where he was, Saxon knew it was J. T. Harris talking.

Well, at least he's here. The trip wasn't for nothing.

"I knew you'd come," the voice through the loudspeakers continued. "You've sought out your one dear friend to commemorate the death of Ellen Hayes."

Furiously now, Saxon started on.

"And we'll celebrate a gala, solemn high mass of black magic for it," the voice coming from the different horns boomed. "Feats of legerdemain that will astound even your jaded and perceptive eyes."

Saxon stopped, cupped his hands to yell for J. T. to show himself, but didn't, realized it would be useless; the millionaire was playing a child's game, and Saxon was sure he wouldn't let anyone spoil it.

Maybe he *had* flipped. It could be that Nick Serano was right in his judgment.

But why? What was the root of J. T.'s sickness?

Murder?

Had he killed Ellen in a moment of frustration and rage because she refused to sell him a secret she didn't really know?

Was this a last stand?

A final defiance before his inevitable arrest for a crime he had been unable to prevent himself from committing?

"For I possess illusions you have never dreamed possible." Rasping through tin hollows of acoustic sound, J. T.'s voice now seemed angry.

Saxon started walking again, and approached the outdoor bar. It stood open, glasses and bottles on the shelves, a blue and white awning giving shade to the red, leather-topped bar stools. One of the speakers was attached inside.

"It will be a festival of magic, Mr. Saxon. Mine. I'm laying down the gauntlet. I challenge you to the title of 'greatest.' "

Saxon unlatched the half door, walked behind the bar, gazing at the stock to choose ingredients for a drink.

"Fastest sleight-of-hand on earth," J. T.'s voice said, beginning to rage. "This is the showdown."

Yes, he's flipped, Saxon thought, mixing himself a drink and dropping cubes of ice in it.

"May the best man inherit the title of Conjurer Supreme."

Saxon lifted his drink as a toast to that.

"And this time," the loudspeaker voice crackled, almost in his ear, "you won't stand there with a smug look identifying the origin of each illusion: 'Chevalier Pinetti, 1796,' 'Bantier de Kolter, 1875.' "

Saxon shrugged, sipped his drink.

And understood now why the Lida illusion had become such an absolute obsession for J. T. He wanted to own all there was of magic, and since he, in fact, already almost did, his collector's zeal had been thwarted. "Lida" meant more to a man like him than the Mona Lisa. It was an art treasure beyond his grasp.

"The pool, Joe. Quickly, quickly. The swimming pool. I think I'm going to drown."

Saxon put down his glass, came out from behind the bar

and started to the swimming pool. He did not run. A magician's trick begins with deception and it was possible this was a feint to get him away from the bar.

He was within fifteen feet of that clear, blue body of water glistening in the late afternoon sun when he heard the sound of a gunshot. He looked quickly around, then hearing a hiss, up. A clay pigeon was in the air over his head. There was the sound of a second shot, and a moment later the disc shattered.

Saxon felt foolish that he had experienced a twinge of concern, and turning back to the swimming pool, stared incredulously.

It was empty.

Then he chuckled. The gunshots, the clay pigeon had been the feint to draw his attention. The wizard deftly directs your eyes away, and when you look back, presto, the illusion is accomplished. Shades of Mandrake the Great, he thought. The pool obviously had a false bottom. As Saxon diverted his gaze, it had slid swiftly back, depositing the water into a second bottom, then slid to again. However, it was clever, showed almost maniacal ingenuity, because there had been no sound of splashing, no massive thump of a ton of water plunging below.

Must have cost you pretty good to have that installed. Of course it was built to amaze your friends. There hasn't been time to devise it for my benefit. But bravo, anyway. I give you credit for firing the first shot in the "showdown."

And Saxon remembered another time, another place, a different millionaire, one who had no interest in magic whatsoever, but whose house (one of many houses he owned and frequented) was rigged with trick doors, one of them hidden behind a medicine cabinet in the bathroom that led to a secret, hidden room. But the real *tour de force* in that rich man's playhouse in the hills outside Pasadena had been truly amazing. Managing to distract the attention of his guests by pointing up at a mural on the ceiling of the living room and giving a little discourse on the intricacies of it, he pressed a button that slowly lowered the entire floor—including that ceiling you were concentrating on—to a rumpus room bar one story below.

Saxon remembered the shock he had felt at suddenly seeing different surroundings. He was twelve that year and it was the "keenest" thing he'd ever known. He talked about it for years, vowing he would some day install a sinking room into a house of his own. But of course he never had. There were so many things he had promised himself and it now all seemed long ago in the Land of Nod.

"Go ahead, Joe," the loudspeakers all intoned, "tell me how *that* was done and who invented it."

Saxon realized for the first time that wherever J. T. was, he was drunk.

He looked up, lifting his arms as if in a gesture to say he *didn't* know how the trick was done.

J. T. Harris had at last trapped him into viewing one of his performances.

"Mr. Saxon," the voice intoned, "start up the walk toward the hotel."

Saxon obeyed, moved up the walk, but soon stopped. A small circle of ground ahead of him was erupting chunks of earth. Then, as he stood there, a tree began to appear, a banana tree. Up, up it came, a few inches, than a foot at a time, until it was fully grown, red bananas hanging from its leafy branches.

Saxon smiled. Okay, J. T., levitation of a banana tree out of the ground.

Gad, sir, astounding.

But some of the earth had fallen away from the metal plate that had elevated the tree upward.

Has the devotion to things magic degenerated to this?

"And who invented *that*?" the loudspeakers shrieked in unison.

No professional would have been crude enough to let telltale metal expose his enchanted-appearing tree, he wanted to tell him.

Then, through the loudspeakers, unscheduled, there was the crash of a breaking bottle.

The bar in the Turtle Lounge.

Saxon started toward the lounge, but suddenly heard a loud, wailing scream, and staring in the distance, saw a large guillotine, the figure of a woman kneeling, her neck on the chopping block, a glistening curved blade poised above, a giant executioner ready to release it. Though a rigged guillotine is also a magician's stock in trade, Saxon did as he was expected—ran toward the contraption. Halfway there he heard a *swoosh*. The blade came clattering down, the woman's head cleaved off, dropped into a basket, arteries of blood spurting everywhere; and the executioner stood back, gurgling gleefully.

Arriving at the guillotine, Saxon, out of breath, saw at once the "woman" had been a mannequin, the blood was red paint, and the still burbling executioner was constructed of plastic, a toy of some kind inside his head producing the noise that came out of his mouth.

In a fit of pettish frenzy, Saxon hoisted up the blade, secured it, then grabbed the dummy of the executioner, slammed it down, its neck in the curved rack, and let the blade fall. The plastic head plopped into the basket on top of the mannequin head and wallowed in red paint, the noise that had emanated from it now a *whir* of tiny, clashing wheels.

Entering the Turtle Lounge, Saxon saw that it was empty; fish nets, seashells, the glittering bar, straight chairs that still faced the small stage at the far end of the room. Moving slowly now, he came on in, and then the curtains opened on stage, and he saw J. T. Harris up there, clad in the conjurer's traditional garb of coattails and top hat. He was holding a black bird-cage in front of him. There was a canary inside.

"Welcome, Mr. Saxon," J. T. said. "The performance will now continue."

Saxon was ready to shout invectives at him, but the amateur magician was drunk, weaving, and in the next instant was also ludicrous: he held the cage too far out and the canary escaped, flying in circles around the room, then crashing into a wall, knocking itself out. J. T. apparently hadn't noticed. With a flourish, he released the cage. It disappeared, all right, but snapped back against him so hard it bowled him over.

Scrambling to his feet, reaching for the top hat, dusting it off and putting it back on his head, he bowed nonetheless, and under ordinary circumstances Saxon wouldn't have known whether to applaud, laugh or start crying.

Obviously working without an assistant, J. T. now produced a deck of cards, talking as he fumbled, desperately trying to set up the next trick.

"I know why you're here."

Saxon didn't think it necessary to answer. Let him go on.

"But I *did* send the telegram out as I promised. I *did* do that. I removed the danger she was in."

He teetered at the edge of the stage, the cards slipping from his grasp. J. T. got down on his hands and knees, pitifully scooping them up.

"But there's no law says I can't buy something I want. Even if it *isn't* for sale."

He somehow gained his feet once more, fanning the cards.

"So when I found out Ellen Hayes was in New Orleans, I arranged to do a show there, and hired her for one night as my assistant."

He sailed the cards out, but in this light the threads designed to draw them gracefully back in were not invisible, and even more embarrassing, he got them tangled in his fingers. The cards fell to the floor below the stage and he reeled them in like fish on a line. He sensed by now the act was a flop, and was almost crying. Yet had that sudden surge of grief been brought on simply because he had failed to entertain his guest? Saxon thought not.

"Something you *don't* know, Saxon." The words were beginning to slur, and J. T. Harris was now thoroughly exhausted from the intricate game he had been playing. "Damn it, I need a drink."

He dropped the threaded cards, staggered to the side of the stage and precariously navigated steps to the floor, heading straight to the bar. Again Saxon wanted to speak but detected that J. T. was neither hearing or seeing too well; best to let him talk, get it all out, whatever it was that was burdening him.

"I brought a check along to New Orleans in the amount of one hundred thousand dollars, made out to her. In the upper left hand corner was the word 'Lida.' The *name* Lida? I presented it to her after the performance. She just frowned, seemed suddenly nervous, tore it in half and handed it back."

He was hanging on the side of the bar now, immersed in emotion, and evidently forgetting he had come for a drink.

"She was so fresh and different," he said, "and I'm accustomed to such eighteen-carat phonies, I almost couldn't stand it. Tear up a check for more money than she'd probably ever see in a lifetime? It was a profound shock. And just beautiful. I think I started to cry or something. They really *made* girls like that? Well, what you *don't* know is, the next thing I tried to buy was her." He began shouting, bloodshot eyes looking past Saxon. "I wasn't interested in your frigging, crap-out illusion any more. I wanted *her*."

He lost his grip on the bar, stumbled out to the middle of the small dance floor, banging into a row of the straight chairs facing the stage. But at last got his balance, and his voice low now, no longer addressed to Saxon, went on:

"I asked her to marry me."

He was still for a moment, considering the holy wonder of that. He had asked a woman he'd known but a few hours to be his wife.

"And she said 'thank you, but no.' 'Why?' I asked her. 'I don't love you.' 'What,' I asked, 'does that have to do with it? I'm offering you the world. Gift wrapped.' " Aware again that Saxon was there listening, "And her answer was 'I love someone else.' And guess who, Saxon? Guess who, you son-of-a-bitch?" He propelled himself back to the bar, this time going around behind it. "So—of all the things I am most unlikely to do, I did the unlikely." Voice louder. "I spent the next ten minutes of my life being a half-assed decent human being." He reached for a bottle, but it slipped from his hand and broke as it hit the floor, mingling with the pieces of a bottle he had broken earlier. J. T. blithely reached for a new one. "I told her 'he loves you, too.' She didn't believe it, hadn't known it, even guessed, and I yelled at her 'he *told* me he was in love with you, and right now that bastard is searching for you'; and she started crying and said, 'He won't have to search any more, I'll find *him*, I'll go to him,' and she kissed me because I had told her."

He poured a straight shot of whiskey.

"Ellen kissed me," he said, the mottled, drunken face sad. Then he looked up at Saxon. "She was going to leave the next day and go to San Francisco and find you, but she didn't make it through life as far as the next day." The voice was raging. "And you're here because you think I'm such a slob I might have killed her. I know—they've arrested somebody, but that wouldn't mean anything to you. You've never liked me, never had any respect at all, and I realize how it looks that I was in New Orleans on the night of the murder. But I didn't—"

His voice was choked. Lifting the straight shot, he gulped it down.

"If the man under arrest isn't the guilty party, it has to be one of those little creeps that think magic is the fountain of all creation." He paused. "Like I did once. And still do. How'd you like my disappearing swimming pool? I've had fun with it. And the guillotine. Isn't that the most real thing you've ever seen? We've had women faint over that. And I swear, Saxon, they're my own invention. Not that I invented the guillotine, but the way I had it set up. And the banana tree, too. I'm not the dumb cluck playboy you think I am." His voice trailed off, his thoughts seeming to wander, and he came back to:

"It was that little, crawly clubfoot with the magic shop in East St. Louis who called to tell me she was in New Orleans. Took him a week to get through to me, but he managed it. He wanted a commission if I was successful in buying the Lida illusion."

Saxon took a long, last look at J. T. Harris and realized that in regard to Ellen every word he had spoken was true.

Make things right.

He had wasted his time.

XX

IF PARENTS were alarmed by the possible damaging effects certain war toys might have on the minds of children, The Chinese Water Torture Trick, invented by Eli Wheeler, would have outraged them beyond reason. By his own admission, sales had been poor, but returns to the stores where the "game" had been purchased were probably staggering. It consisted of canvas binds for wrists and ankles, an inverted fish bowl with a hole in it to be erected overhead from which water dripped one drop at a time, and various instruments of torture—a needlepoint dagger, pliers for pulling out teeth, fingernails or eyelids, a small cleaver to cut off ears or nose, and other diabolic fantasia: all harmless, of course, made of rubber, but hideous in appearance. The rules were quite simple. Each child, or adult ("adults will delight in the game") would take turns as the "victim," lying flat, arms and legs bound, the arms preferably held above the head. In addition to the slow drip-drip of water ("on the forehead, or whatever other sensitive area of the body, to be agreed upon by the players"), participants would pretend to inflict excruciating pain with the play items of torture. The "victim" able to remain inert and silent for the longest duration of time was declared winner.

An endurance contest. ("One outcry or violent movement within a three-minute period automatically disqualifies the player," the rules warned, and went on to add: "If there is no winner, the game will immediately commence again, and once more happy shrieks of laughter will fill the room.")

Saxon had deftly admitted himself through the back door of the magic shop in East St. Louis at five in the morning, and The Chinese Water Torture Trick had been the first thing he examined. He knew that Eli Wheeler was a devious little man who could not be dealt with in a usual manner. He would lie up to his last gasp of breath. Magic alone filled him with wonder, and if certain feats could be cleverly brought off, the demonstration might tip the scales of his normal rationale. If he had harmed Ellen before her death (and someone had), Saxon couldn't go to the police in this city and make such a charge. Even if he could be located, Professor not very Marvelous George Dekker wouldn't appear as a witness against him, and certainly Ellen couldn't. It was a moot question whether the lovely wraith even demanded police action.

Saxon felt if it was possible to force the clubfoot to admit his guilt, spew out a confession as to what had occurred in Las Vegas, it might satisfy her. Though not, of course, if it had been he who was guilty of her murder. Saxon doubted whether he had ever been in New Orleans. Yet it was possible. Anything was possible. It was not up to him to guess, but find out all that had gone on, and insofar as humanly possible try to right the wrong and/or wrongs she had suffered.

Saxon did not have the props with him necessary for the performance of truly great magic, nor would he wait until they could be shipped, so he was going to have to work with small devices he had in the secret linings of his coat, and anything else he could improvise here on the spot with what meagre material there was on hand. It would be difficult, because Eli Wheeler was a superior afficionado, and hard to deceive.

He put The Chinese Water Torture Trick on the counter, and searching the place, discovered the stored-away little Santa Claus that had appeared in the front window during the holidays. He lifted it from its musty resting place, and looking around, found a box of "funny putty," an item that was for sale on one of the shelves. Then, discovering "invisible" thread in a box that offered still another parlor trick, he set to work, stopping now and then to think and then hunt for other useful novelties.

At eight-thirty, Eli Wheeler limped up to the glass street door of the narrow, hole-in-the-wall magic shop. Saxon stood in shadows beside the wooden door at the opposite end. The clubfoot unlocked the front door, came in, a little bell tinkling as the door closed again. He seemed weary, depressed at the start of day's business. It was cold outside and he had on a topcoat which he now removed. He started to the back room with it.

Suddenly seeing Saxon, he stopped abruptly, peering, wondering whether he was imagining it, worried and cross with himself that it might be an hallucinatory vision; then, realizing it *was* Saxon, his furtive eyes suddenly darted about, as if seeking a way of escape.

Then, as Saxon anticipated he would, he put down his topcoat and like a small animal backed to the wall, showing its long teeth, tried to brazen it out.

"You—you broke in here, Mr. Saxon."

Saxon's black, piercing eyes concentrated all of their power into Wheeler's eyes, and though Saxon had each night in the theater experienced momentary success at mass hypnosis, he could not pin the little man into anything that began to be a trance.

"He told you, didn't he? That I called him?"

"J. T. told me."

"Familiar with him, aren't you? 'J. T.' Well, if you only knew how badly he wanted 'Lida—' "

"He didn't kill Ellen Hayes."

"*He* say that?" Eli Wheeler began gimping around, no longer letting his eyes meet the strength of Saxon's. "And you believed him? Well, well."

"I want to know what happened in Las Vegas."

"Nothing. I told you when you were here before. *Nothing.* Now just what the hell are you doing here in my place? Breaking in like a common thief. Tell me *that. You* answer questions for a change."

"I've come to perform for you," Saxon said.

"You're wasting your time." Ferret eyes still looking for a hole to crawl into.

"First, The Chinese Water Torture Trick."

"I should call the police. *Tell* them you broke in."

Saxon pointed at a shelf, and as Wheeler turned to look little curtains parted and a doll, a foot long, with a pretty face, blonde hair worn at one side, was visible, nude, The Chinese Water Torture Trick rigged above her, drops of water slowly splashing her body, but in a ghastly addition to the "game": knives, forks and spoons (the kind that collapsed if you tried to eat with them, har har) dangled above, in mid-air, darting down, as if to slice or puncture the doll, the doll's head rising up, falling back, rising up, falling back, as if in horror.

Gaping, the clubfoot at last found his voice.

"My trick. You're using my little children's game."

"A *children's* game?"

Eli Wheeler was dancing about, from the clubfoot to the normal eyes fastened on the realistic image made by the doll.

"Children love those kind of things. They're little animals.

Tiny monsters. Didn't you know that? They are happiest while inflicting punishment. Cruelty is their nature. They are born with that in them. But adults stifle it." Shrieking, as the game rules promised, but not laughter. "Let them go, I say, unbridled, in an innocent little game where they can rid themselves of those desires. It was a favor to humanity, that invention." Now concerned at the apparatus. "What have you done to it? How did you make that?"

He ran behind the counter, peered at the doll, the head still rising up, falling back, then in seething rage began shouting:

"My little Santa Claus I've used for the past five years. You've stripped off its face and made a new one of putty. You've torn away its red costume, simulating a woman's body, and plugged in the mechanism that moves it." He reached out for the knives, forks and spoons, but they skipped away from him, raised up to the ceiling. Eli Wheeler stared up, grinding his teeth, then the darting little eyes took in Saxon. "*You're* doing that. I'm up on the latest sophisticated devices, Saxon, I know about the magnetic ray."

As if deflated at having been exposed, Saxon disappeared the magnetic ray into the lining of his coat, and the knife, fork and spoon plummeted to the floor.

"See, I told you," Wheeler screeched.

But coming out from behind the counter, he was clearly unnerved, and at once, in the back room, something even more disturbing began to occur. A *poof*, then a misty, shimmering body of white appeared.

"She's here," Saxon said.

The clubfoot stared, trembling. "I don't believe it. I've been around magic and magicians all my life. I know you people."

"You tortured her, beat her."

"No, no, that's a damned lie."

In a frenzy, he gimped up to the luminous light, and then as if going crazy, began to croak: "You scraped the phosphorous from the faces of my masks. You constructed this, you constructed it . . ."

That was true, and when the mist evaporated, Eli Wheeler turned in triumph.

"If you are quite through with your amazing feats of leger-demain, Mr. Saxon—"

I'll never make things right, Saxon thought.

This little bastard is too sharp.

But all at once a white shroud swirled into the atmosphere, and there was a low, growling, humming sound.

Eli Wheeler stumbled about, gazing at it. "Think you can fool me again?"

The clubfoot struck out with his fists at empty air, fanned at the whirling white cone, but the ghost came at him, drove him back, now too real to doubt, too horrifying to even contemplate. Wheeler gazed at Saxon who looked on, unperturbed. Ellen had said if she could she would help him.

"Saxon, for the love of God, stop doing this."

"I'm not doing it."

Eli Wheeler clumped back into the main part of the shop, the ghost following, a whining sound now. The clubfoot fell against the counter.

"Saxon, what is it you want?"

"Truth."

Suddenly almost unaware of the ghost, staring only at Saxon, the little man's eyes widened.

"It's true what so many believe. You *have* acquired the art of black magic."

"Truth," Saxon demanded.

"It's true, it's true," hysterical ecstasy, "you've crossed the line."

"Truth."

"Yes, in Las Vegas we used The Chinese Water Torture Trick on her. *I* used it."

The ghost was quiet now, moving to and fro, as if listening. Eli Wheeler watched it, his yellow teeth showing as his mouth worked.

"We needed money. George and I always need money, and she was the answer." He raged inwardly. "Everything, every time is always going to be the God-damned answer." He got back to the subject. "But Ellen Hayes wasn't interested in our problem. She fought us like a cat, and I hit her, I had to. She was knocked out and we took her to George's room at Rainbow's End, the room he kept on the side, and when she came to we had her racked out for The Chinese Water Torture Trick. We weren't going to hurt her or anything. You *know* it's harmless. We were just going to scare her into talking."

"Racked her out how?"

He lowered his head. "The trick is always more effective if
—"

"You stripped her clothes off."

"Yes." Wheeler didn't notice, but the wraith now vanished. "She wouldn't say a single word, and after a while I got mad—"

"And hit her again."

"Yes, I hit her with my cane." He was frothing, staring into thin air at what he now imagined was the ghost. "I didn't want to do it, but you made me. You wouldn't say anything, not anything, except to call out *his* name, 'Joe . . . Joe,' think he could hear you?"

At the airport, ready to board a flight for Hong Kong; I heard her then when she was battered and hurting and needed me.

"I heard her," Saxon said.

But Eli Wheeler was no longer hearing anything.

"She's gone," Saxon told him.

The clubfoot didn't hear that, either. Or if he had, refused to believe it; he was still "seeing" that which he did not, believing Saxon had indeed conjured up Ellen's ghost from the beyond, and more than that, had long possessed that uncanny ability, and being as Saxon had ascribed, a superior afficionado, it drove a fear into his heart greater than a pike into that of a Dracula in a coffin. It was not the wraith he still thought he saw that he feared, but Saxon. Eli Wheeler who had followed magic and adored its wizards all his whole life was now a True Believer of the greatest he had ever heard of or known.

Saliva appeared at the corners of his teeth-gritting mouth, his eyes rolled in awe, and again looking at Saxon, he was gibbering, a poor subject mentally kneeling at the confessional on High.

"I didn't want to hurt her, sir, but would have, I was so frantic." Abject now, truth, truth, God knows all anyway, don't try to fool Him, it will only incur His wrath. "However, George stopped me. George, that pipsqueak womanizer, so sentimental about them. He dragged me back, away from her, and when I was calm again, we released her of the bonds of my simple little children's game. And we left her there, we left her, I honestly didn't mean to hurt her."

"But did."

"I see now, Mr. Saxon, now that she is dead, she is the goddess of magic, and I have known—oh, God, do you realize what it's been like for me—that young boy who once aspired to be a wizard, like you, and couldn't, with a limp? The agony of it, the frustration, yet following magic, reading its history, worshipping its masters, though, sir, there has never been one who has attained *your* powers."

"Did you kill her?"

"Oh, no, no, though if J. T. Harris is guilty, I am instrumental, surely, I called him. Yes, I told him she was probably in New Orleans. But it was George Dekker who informed me she would be there next. She had said to him a day or two before she could find employment there at some department store, and though George is a gentle person he was more desperate for the money than I."

Gentle? Saxon had interrupted Professor Marvelous in an act of murder.

Eli Wheeler was wringing his hands. "What is to be my punishment?"

Saxon blanked out his mind, waiting for the answer, and when it did not come, replied:

"You are condemned to live with yourself for the rest of your life."

XXI

THOUGH it was rumored he was in San Francisco, the truth was nobody, anywhere, knew exactly where George Dekker might be found; Professor Marvelous had evidently waved his magic wand and "disappeared" himself, which drove Saxon to an even stronger belief that he must see him. He was, to say the least, responsible in part for the suffering Ellen had been compelled to endure, and it might prove out he was even more deeply involved than that. But how to trace a man who, to all appearances, was in hiding? How except by the uncanny, dark power of mind Saxon had sought through the years and now had at last achieved.

Or had he? Were the breakthroughs so far attained by sheer energized concentration on the one singular quest to reach Ellen? Could he grope blindly out into the void and pinpoint an alien, unwilling subject? But what of the queer sensations he had experienced Christmas Eve waiting through the long night at the airport in New Orleans? The personal column of that newspaper he had read, his inner mind probing out tingling feelers into the dusty human hearts of people he had never met, and would never meet. Strangers. It could have been imagined. Or it might be, as he had reflected then, that he was mad, therefore gifted, because only the insane know truth.

However, whatever, he was here in his baroque apartment in San Francisco, that big, lonely barn Marge had called a museum; and was seated, eyes closed, absorbed in total, intense effort, the radar of his subconscious searching, hunting through darkness, but poised, magnetized to zero in on the magician whose face was as seamed as a baseball, whose pencil-line moustache had wriggled up and down like rabbit whiskers that sad, awful, tragi-comic night in Las Vegas when wife Dana jammed the top hat over his face. A comedy with tears. Professor Marvelous insisting right up to the end the show had to go on. Find him, put traits and facets of him together, make a whole man to which a psyche can respond.

And after a while Saxon grew tense, his mind seemed swirling; little streaks of light shot arrows into the pitch black out there; the glow of the arrows died and were eaten by darkness, yet reappeared again, zinging every which way, sparkling pinwheels of light. It was as though his fingertips were on the indicator of an Ouija board that had suddenly gone crazy, going zig-zag, here, there, then Saxon heard himself gasp for he saw the flash image of George Dekker suspended upside down, arms and legs grotesquely askew, glassy dead eyes hanging open in abject terror. Then it was gone, vanished into a fetid, airless tomb.

Tomb. Tomb. Saxon held fast to the word. Then all at once realized he could not breathe. He was in a casket with Professor Marvelous and there was no air. Oh, Jesus, God, I'm suffocating, and he remembered that summer so long ago when they were doing one-day stands and it was raining and the lid of the coffin fell in on him and the emergency cord to signal he was in trouble was stuck.

Struggling without breath, he tried now to reach out for such a cord, but there was none there, there was nothing there, and a band of steel was beginning to crush his chest.

But like a cork bursting from the mouth of a bottle, he popped out of that dank enclosure, breathing air again, eyes still closed, and saw a simple, inexpensive grave marker with the name George Dekker on it; and kneeling by that fresh grave was a small, pretty woman, and she was crying, truly heartbroken sobs being wrung from her. A moment before that scene faded, Saxon noticed the bay in the distance, and recognized the cemetery.

He broke the trance, and within minutes left the apartment.

He was approaching the cemetery gate when he saw Dana Dekker coming out, looking forlorn, petite in her black dress, and the black veil she wore over her head. Saxon reached her, but it was a moment before she recognized him. Then when she did, was very bitter.

"It's your fault he's dead. That damn girl of yours."

"Could we go somewhere and talk?"

"I don't *want* to talk to you, Mr. Saxon. There's nothing to say any more about anything."

It was Saxon's turn to be bitter. "That 'damn girl' of mine. She's dead, too, you know."

Dana gazed up at him for a moment, her veil riffled by a cold wind blowing in off the bay.

"Yes," she said, "I'm sorry. It's all such a terrible—and it *wasn't* your fault, God knows. George brought it on himself. He never once told me anything about it. He was too ashamed. Then that night John Turk came over and—" She began crying, "—that's when I learned what had happened to poor Ellen. How much money they thought they would get from—" She broke off. "But she was gone by then, by the time Mr. Turk came over. She was going back to New Orleans."

"Turk knew that?"

"Of course. George didn't leave out one single detail."

Saxon touched her arm. "I hear that you put up a pretty good fight yourself." He was attempting in some small way to assuage just a bit of her grief. "Jumped on Turk's back, bit him —"

"I didn't put up a good enough fight," Dana said. Then, seeing Saxon didn't seem to understand, went on: "Why do you think George is dead?"

Saxon felt stupid that it hadn't occurred to him to ask. "You're telling me he never recovered from the beating?"

"No, he never did. He was all broken up inside. I got him into a hospital up here. The *city* hospital. That's because we didn't have enough money to pay for—at least not enough. He died yesterday, and was buried today. I *did* pay for that." The tears that had stopped for just a moment came again, harder. "Mr. Saxon, I was the only one at the funeral."

"You loved him despite everything."

"Yes."

"You're a remarkable woman, Dana."

"I'm a remarkable nothing. All I have is a remarkably cute little can. Who'll I show it to now?"

"May I give you a lift somewhere?"

She nodded. "To the Department of Employment. Or is it closed at this hour?"

She was staying at a shabby hotel on Market Street. Driving her there, Saxon said:

"Please don't leave town or go anywhere until you hear from me."

She looked up. "Why?"

"Now that George is dead the case of assault you could have had against Turk is changed. It's murder. You want him to go scot free?"

Her face hardened. She was, if nothing else, totally vindictive. "No. No, I don't."

"Let me handle it."

He dropped her at the hotel, returned to his apartment, and phoned the best detective agency in town. They had an office in Las Vegas and promised immediate investigative action.

Just minutes over one hour later, a call came from the Nevada town. Airline records showed a John Turk had booked passage from Las Vegas to New Orleans (via San Francisco) on December 29th. Saxon thanked the private detective and hung up.

He sat there for a moment, excited, angry. *He* had called Turk on January 10th, listening to him boast how he had beaten up George Dekker, a man half his size. A boast he said he had described to Ellen when she called to ask whether there was any chance to return to her job at Rainbow's End. Turk had told her "no," whether the chance existed or not, evidently because he planned to come after her himself and it wouldn't do to have that meeting with her (particularly if violence might be involved) in his own backyard. He had ascertained she was on her way to New Orleans, and a day or two later, followed her to that city.

J. T. Harris had sent telegrams withdrawing his monetary offer for the Lida illusion; but Turk, not on the list of magicians and their afficionados, had not received one, so had no way of knowing he was pursuing a prize no longer available.

Saxon felt positive he had found the killer, but didn't know which way to move next. He badly needed professional help.

He put in a call to New Orleans.

"Nick, you told me when I thought I had something to give you a holler."

"Thanks, buddy boy," the homicide cop said over the wire, "but *I* now have something. Our friend the department store executive made a tentative confession. Going to have to spend the next couple of days going over it with him to plug up the holes—but he's nailed."

"Said yourself he might confess to get you off his back."

"—Then recant at the trial. Well, *let* him."

"I gather from that," Saxon said, "you're not interested in any other possible suspect. You've already got one, and whether he's guilty or not, you're going to crucify him."

"Whoa, back up."

"I'd sure as hell hate to have you after *me*. Particularly if innocent. It'd scare the crap out of me."

"Joe—"

"A confession with holes in it," Saxon raged, "and a possible recant at the trial. When you gamble, you go all the way, don't you? Well, it so happens *I* have more at stake in this than becoming the next D.A. of New Orleans."

"Joe, God damn it—" A pause, then: "You have *what* at stake? What the hell do *you* have at stake?"

"You don't believe in ghosts," Saxon said, "so I wouldn't expect you to understand."

"Oh." Followed by silence.

"Besides," Saxon went on, "I think you forget that I've been guided by certain instincts in this case that so far have proved out one hundred per cent."

"Yes, you found the body, if that's what—your instinct tells you Perry Cole isn't our boy?

"Just forget it."

"No," Nick Serano said, "I'll do everything I can. The big point is, I think I'm right, you think you are. But I certainly want to see it through. You're implying I'm not a thorough cop, and I resent that."

"The suspect I have in mind is already guilty of one provable murder. Complete with an eye-witness. It was assault. I doubt he knows the victim died."

"Guy sounds rough."

"A rough, remorseless toad, and capable of anything you can name. And I guess you realize he's not in your jurisdiction. Nick, who do you know in Las Vegas?"

"Nobody." It was now Nick who was a little sarcastic, "But in the past we law enforcement people *have* been known to work together. Fill me in on the details. I'll call the Sheriff there, then grab a plane and we can meet anywhere you say."

At ten the next morning Saxon, Nick Serano and big, sun-tanned, gray-headed Sheriff Wayne Rogers of Las Vegas showed up in Turk's office, uninvited and unannounced. The big, obese, bald booking agent leaned back in his chair, a cigar jammed in his mouth. Around the four walls the eyes of all the girls in the glossy eight by ten pictures seemed to be watching him intently, though not with concern; and outside, on the street one story below, throngs of losers marched a rag-tag parade in the never-ending human pursuit of quick, easy riches.

Turk said brightly: "To what do I attribute, as the saying goes?"

Sheriff Rogers introduced Nick Serano. "And I believe you know Joe Saxon."

"I've met him," Turk said, unimpressed. "But what the hell's a police lieutenant from New Orleans doing here?"

"Few questions," Wayne Rogers told him coldly, "which may lead to a request for extradition papers that'll get you a free ride to Louisiana. But first," he began the tired police chant, "I must warn you, you are entitled to have an attorney present—"

Turk was on his feet, punching out the cigar in an ashtray. "Never mind that crap. I don't know what you're talking about."

"Your recent visit to our city," Nick Serano said.

"I've never been to New Orleans in my life."

Both Wayne Rogers and Nick looked over at Saxon. Saxon produced a copy of the airline ticket and handed it to Turk, who stared, then sat down heavily.

"All right, so I was there."

"To see Ellen Hayes," Saxon said.

"No, it was business."

"Turk, your business is here," Sheriff Rogers snapped, "don't tell us you went to New Orleans looking for talent."

"God damn it, I don't have to tell you anything."

"He's right he was there on business," Nick said, "because he'd found out how much certain information might be worth —information he thought Ellen Hayes had."

"Sure I found out," Turk admitted, fuming, "but it didn't mean nothing to me. I'm not in the magic business."

"You found out," Rogers pounded, "the night you beat up George Dekker."

It was like dealing from a cold deck, but it worked. Turk was rattled now. "That creep had it coming."

"So have you," the Las Vegas Sheriff said. He took a document from his pocket and laid it on the desk. "Warrant for your arrest. The charge is murder."

Turk's bloated face was stricken. "You gotta be kidding."

"George Dekker died day before yesterday," the gray-haired, sun-tanned Sheriff said. "His wife signed the complaint this morning."

Turk looked at the three of them, from one face to the other. It appeared he wanted to get up from the chair again, but didn't have the strength. It was the correct psychological moment for Nick Serano to pounce.

"*Now* you want to tell us about your trip to New Orleans?"

"You might as well," Sheriff Rogers urged Turk. "Because you'll get the death penalty for Dekker's murder, that I guarantee. We don't tolerate your kind of hooliganism and mayhem in Nevada, and we'll make damn sure the rest of the world knows that."

Turk was shaking.

"You have nothing more to lose," Saxon said. "You murdered Ellen Hayes, didn't you?"

"Hell, no, I didn't." Turk's voice was now thundering. He hit his fist on the desk. "I went there to talk to her, yes. But I didn't even do that. Figured it wouldn't be necessary because I ran into that young punk who kept standing in front of the department store window hours at a time while she was performing."

Saxon suddenly recalled the familiar figure he had seen on the sidewalk before the window on the day he himself had been there, his astral body permitted but a few fleeting moments. Grant Sawyer.

"I got talking to him," Turk went on, "and found out he'd been her sweetheart once and still was panting for her, out of his skull wanting her back."

"Grant Sawyer," Nick said. He'd done his homework on the case.

"Yeah—him," Turk affirmed, "only he worked in a gas station or somewhere, didn't have a chance with that broad, anyway didn't think he did; so I took him up the street to a bar and pitched him on how he *could* have a chance. Money would do it, I told him, and he was in a better position than anybody to get some fast. All he had to do was pump the secret of Saxon's magic act out of her."

"And turn it over to you," Nick Serano said.

"Yeah—I'd sell it to that Florida millionaire, and me and the kid'd split up a hundred G's."

"Turk," Saxon said, "you may have met Grant Sawyer, but he wouldn't have harmed Ellen. It was you."

"Hell it was me." Turk was shouting so loudly the secretary came in from the outer office to see whether anything was the matter. "Get out of here," he bellowed at her, and when she quickly retreated, turned to Saxon, and lowering his voice continued: "You got a duplicate of that airline ticket I bought here. S'matter, didn't you check out the return ticket I picked up in New Orleans? I was back here in my office on January 3rd."

Ellen had been murdered early on the morning of January 6th.

Nick Serano lifted the telephone and called the airlines desk in New Orleans. While waiting for the information, he looked over at Sheriff Rogers.

"Go ahead, take him in on the Dekker murder. If his story checks out on the day he left New Orleans we won't be bothering you any more."

"Come on, Turk," Wayne Rogers said.

John Turk lumbered to his feet, reached for the dead stogie in the ashtray, then put it back again.

Five minutes later, only Saxon and Nick Serano remained in the office. Nick at last hung up the phone, and Saxon read the answer on his face.

"Sorry, Joe. He wasn't in New Orleans the night of the murder."

Saxon leaned back against the desk, stunned, quiet, brooding; Nick lit a cigarette, walked over and put it in Saxon's mouth.

"As I told you, Joe, one of us was right, the other had to be wrong. Trouble is, you rely too much on thinking you're mystic."

"All right, I was wrong on Turk," Saxon said. "But what about Grant Sawyer? You just going to forget *he* had a motive?"

"We're both going to have to forget him," the homicide cop said gently. "He committed suicide in Baton Rouge on the day of the murder."

XXII

HE HAD REACHED a cul-de-sac of emptiness. There were no more dark corridors to hurry along in search of answers to riddles that now baffled his comprehension. His hours in imitation of a preying mantis looking with dumb insect eyes into a nadir of void mocked with unbearable frustration. It was like butting his head against the immovable wall of mysterious eternity, star-shaped slabs of iron and concrete guarding its hallowed secrets. He no longer dared to invoke his will to open the door of the beyond, it would be to risk all reason, and already teetering on the edge of night, he didn't want to fall into a snake pit of lunacy from which he knew he would never extricate himself.

She had warned he could not again communicate until things were made right; he had tried to make things right and failed; his touch, as in the nightmare, disappearing everything, that ringing alarm clock receding into darkness. And now Ellen, too, about to recede into the great darkness. He would never see her now, even the ghost of her, and wandering his apartment, desolate, wondered whether he ever had. Those moments in Room 1240 at the Royal Orleans Hotel seemed like a distant dream. If Perry Cole had been guilty of her murder she would not have asked Saxon to make things right. She would have been at rest that he was in jail charged with the crime. And if the department store executive was innocent and unjustly convicted in a court of law she would be forever disturbed. She had depended on Saxon, and he had provided no answer.

He once more assumed the mantle of a "silent," confining himself to the apartment, as though he too were a restless ghost, constantly pacing the length and width of his huge tomb; and as the days passed, and he fasted, eating scarcely enough to stay alive, grew giddy, imagining she was here with him, constantly projecting himself back to that brief hour or two in life she had spent under this roof, pressing the button that opened the old, faded theater curtains and set the footlights aglow on that one far wall where a giant mural depicted posters of his magic acts back through two decades.

And then, one day, a week later (or was it longer? he had lost count), he remembered what he had told Ellen as the two of them stood there: the exact words, the precise phrase. And that was the answer. Like all things immense it was quite simple and had been under his nose all this time. My God, I know the way out for Ellen, and that of course means for myself. I can't communicate, I won't even try, but she will realize what it is because I am thinking it, and she knows what I am thinking; she is somewhere in the beyond, watching me, and waiting. She knew the instant I did just now what it is that has to be done. It will be difficult for her, she'll be repelled, but there is no other solution. Or if there is some worthy solution, I can't find it, it's out of my grasp. So *this* must be it.

Now, all at once, hearing nothing, he was conscious of a raging "no," and though he had not pressed the button to make them do so, the velvet curtains drew swiftly closed, the little footlights flickered out. As though it was a titanic struggle with her, he punched the button, opening the curtains. They immediately closed again, even harder, and he turned away, no longer willing to do battle, feeling despair in her rejection, a black gloom that made his head throb.

He could not sleep that night, lay tossing and turning in bed, arguing with darkness, positive he could convince her, and when without his touching it the bed lamp fell to the floor and broke, only smiled. In her anger she was as destructive as any live woman he had ever known. It delighted him. He felt closer to her. He said aloud:

"Ellen, you know it's the only way."

Silence then, as if, in different circumstances, she had run into her room and slammed the door.

In the morning, he broke his fasting, ate a hearty breakfast. Then dressing quickly, left the apartment. When he returned at three in the afternoon, he was followed by two uniformed delivery boys. It had required both of them to carry so many packages. He paid them, and after they were gone, opened the boxes one by one. Dresses, slips, panties, high-heeled shoes, gay little hats—one with a saucy veil—purses, blouses, sweaters, a silver evening bag, a mink stole—all of these things and more, but no bras.

He put the items away, hanging the dresses in a closet, placing the shoes on a rack. It was after six when he finished and he went into the kitchen to prepare a batch of scrambled eggs for his dinner. It was then that he felt her almost at his shoulder. She was crying. He could hear it distinctly. Soft, sniffling crying.

And he realized (but hadn't he in fact known?) it was not funny. What he demanded of her was dread, horror and suffering. He turned off the stove and let the half-cooked eggs grow cold.

Returning to the big, baroque room, he walked to the

immense picture window and looked out into the night. As usual, he had sought an easy way. And anyhow it was sheer rubbish to believe what she had told him in Room 1240, even if *she* had believed it to be true. There was no way she could physically return. And he felt a fool for buying those dresses and all the pretty accessories. A madcap dunce prancing idiotically on the fragile egg shells of a wistful promise made by a murdered woman roasting in the hell of a purgatory.

He understood what he must have known for some time now, that he could no longer do anything right. He bumbled and tripped in every endeavor. He turned back from the window and didn't have any idea what he would try next. Nothing was what he would try, and surely he could succeed at that. He didn't want to pace around the apartment any more, or to even think. Because why, what was the use of it?

And then he was suddenly alert. That soft crying again, and her whisper, so faint he could scarcely hear:

"All right, darling."

Nick Serano met Saxon at the New Orleans Airport at four o'clock the next afternoon.

"Joe, what I'm going to say, I'm not saying lightly, you've lost your mind."

"I'm perfectly aware of that."

"You're God-damn cheerful about it."

"That's because this is either the end of a nightmare, or I'm a full-fledged lunatic." Face very sober now. "I'd like to know which. Either way, it'll be a relief."

"You said we revisit Room 104."

Saxon nodded. "About one A.M., and if what I think is going to happen comes about, hold tight to your chair. Otherwise *you* might leave that room a raving lunatic."

"God," Nick said, "you get spookier all the time."

They stopped at a counter there in the terminal and ordered coffee.

"Skin at the back of my neck is beginning to crawl," Nick complained, "and here it is still broad daylight. You'd better give me some hint. I thought I'd seen the last of that motel room, and if I have to go through anything else—"

He broke off as the coffee cups were set down before them. A soft voice through the loudspeaker was announcing a departure for New York City at Gate 228.

"Whatever I tell you," Saxon said, "you won't believe it. So why bother?"

"To give me time to prepare for what I'm not going to believe."

Saxon quoted his axiom: "There is no such thing as time."

Nick just looked blank, as though he wished he hadn't asked.

"Everything we do, cruel, or kind, thoughtless, or violent," Saxon went on, "is, has and will always be happening. Footprints marking time that never disappear."

"Just tell me what the hell it is you think is going to happen in Room 104."

"If it works out, as you and I watch, the time in that room —not for us, but the two people who were there then, in those moments—will retrogress back to the night of the murder."

Nick gazed down at his coffee, looking pensive. Then, finally shrugged. "After what I've seen in Room 104, who am I to say I don't believe anything else could happen? Even as wild as that. I know one thing, I'll never be the same man I was before all this. Particularly at night, when there's time to think." He looked over. "Damn it, Joe, there are some things a human being isn't meant to know. It doesn't only stagger the mind, it can warp it." He paused. "I suppose I *do* have to be there with you. I couldn't officially take your word anything like that happened. *If* it does. And if it *does*," he went on suddenly, "the image of the man you're going to see in Room 104 will be Perry Cole."

They sat in total darkness at the far end of Room 104; and though each wore a topcoat, they shivered in the cold and waited, conscious that slithering layers of fog outside had wrapped the Starlight Motel in the icy fingers of a shroud. They did not speak, or stir, but hearing a sound, each tensed, until realizing it was only the moan of a boat whistle somewhere out on the river; and then, their hearing sharply honed, detected the tinkle of far-off buoys, and the distant sound of a train rumbling across a wooden bridge.

Minutes crawled past, as if ticking a dirge, and there was only emptiness. Each could hear the other breathing, and for moments at a time tried not to breathe at all, and began to ache from the waiting, grew restless, the room pervaded by a melancholia that tore at them like fingers. The aura of tenants that had inhabited the place before hung like crepe in the atmosphere: the desperate, the lonely. No sweeping of the air even by a giant fan would ever clear that out. It would remain like old, ugly stains forever to pollute this room now abandoned.

Then both men jumped, though without getting up. There was a knock at the door. They gazed toward one another in the darkness, wondering whether it was an interruption from the outside, if one of them should call out and ask who it was, or get up and open the door to see. When the knock sounded again, Nick Serano *did* start to rise, but sat back down, for the odor of musk had returned to Room 104, the cold air became clammy, and a dim light began to fill the room, busy with white dots joggling everywhere, gradually taking form: the bed that had been stripped of all but the mattress when they came in, now had covers on it, pillows, rumpled. There were odds and ends of feminine belongings on top of the dresser.

"Ellen, let me in." A man's voice.

Ellen slowly became visible, clad in baby dolls, blonde hair disarrayed, face looking sleepy.

"Jesus God, Grant, will *you* go away!"

He was evidently outside the door.

"I just want to say goodbye."

"We've said goodbye."

"I'm headed back to ole Baton Rouge."

The image of Ellen was still not entirely clear, but was identifiable, as was her voice. She approached the door.

"Do you have any idea what time it is?"

He sounded pathetic. "I know what time it is in my life, Ellen."

She moved up close to the door. "*You* are *sickening*. You are so maudlin you make me ill."

"Ah'll never bother you again, Ah swear."

She went to the closet, got out a robe, put it on.

"For old times' sake, a goodbye to my girl."

"*I am not your girl.*"

She crossed to the door, opening it. He all but fell inside, and it was obvious now he was drunk, the alcohol lacing and exaggerating his soft Southern accent. He slammed the door shut, and his manner changed.

"Now you see here, little lady, you're going to listen to me. We got the wonderful chance to be everything again. You can't turn your back on that. We get this money, they'll look up to us again, just like before. They'll say, 'There they go, look at 'em, two most beautiful people in Louisiana.'"

She was coldly furious. "*You* are demented."

He wasn't listening. "I planned and schemed a million

things to make it like it used to be for us, and then it fell right into my lap here in New Orleans, and I saw that as a sign. Honey, it is opportunity knocking. It won't ever knock again. We've got to open the door to Mr. Opportunity."

"You mean to Mr. Turk."

He caught her by the arms, but she fought him off.

"Please get out of here."

"No, I'm not getting out of here, girl, and I'm not getting out of your life, not ever. Don't you see, I *need* you. And you need me. We just ain't anything without each other."

"I'm leaving in the morning for San Francisco."

He stumbled back a step or two, gaping at her, his face mottled, pain stabbing little creases in it.

"Joe Saxon."

"Yes, Joe Saxon."

"No . . . no, you ain't going to him, I'll kill him first, I swear, I'll kill that man, and anybody else that tries to take you away from me. Because you are mine. Are you such a fool you can't see that? You and me is the way it's always been, the way it has to be or else nothing's any good. Just because time has passed don't change it any. You think it changes anything? Sweetheart, it don't."

She tried to speak but couldn't get a word in. He was swept away by memory. A little boy still at the fair, clutching a balloon in one hand, cotton candy in the other, lost, but hearing the sweet music of the carousel.

"Remember that Friday afternoon? Tenth of October, I'll never forget, second game of the season. High school band playing away. '*On, on Mission Parish High, on, on we go;* you and the other cheer leaders waving those pompoms. And then the kick-off, and Ah caught the ball five yards behind the goal line, and Ah started to run, zig-zag, all crazy, straight-arming here, gettin' a block there, and Ah *kept* running, right through them enemy players, and Ah went all the way, one hundred and five yards for a touchdown. You were proud of me *that* day, why aren't you now? Ah'm the same grand person I was then."

Tears splashed down his face and she, too, was crying.

"Please, Grant, please go."

He seemed bewildered. The high school band stopped playing. She wasn't jumping up and down, razzle-dazzle, with the pompoms.

"Don't nothing mean nothing? We can be *rich*."

"I don't know the formula for Mr. Saxon's illusion."

"Oh, bull, bullshit, you know. You know it, all right, and you're going to tell me. For your own good you're going to tell me, so we can be together again."

He grabbed at her again, and she tore at him, scratching his face. It was bleeding.

"Darling," he said, "my pretty darling, if I have to beat you, for your own sweet good to make you tell me—"

He came at her, she struggled, and he was suddenly violent, hitting her with his fists. She fell back, sobbing, and he picked her up, fist poised again.

"No . . . NO . . . !"

But he lashed out, pummeling her. She screamed. It seemed to incense him. He tried to speak, but was mute, slobber dripping from the corners of his mouth. She screamed again, and he threw her against the wall, taking hold of her head and slamming it back, blood spurting, streaming from the back of her head through his fingers. A last, shrill, terrified scream, then she was limp, unconscious, but in a frenzy, he held her up, still beating her splattered head against the wall. He was sobbing.

"Don't you understand nothing?"

Suddenly Room 104 was dark again, silent.

Saxon at last got up, groped his way to the bed lamp and turned it on. The room was stripped, the way it had been when they came in.

It was clear to him that the enraged wraith in Room 1240 that had urged him up onto the ledge of the window had been Grant Sawyer.

Now he looked over at Nick Serano who was still seated in the chair by the far wall, face drained white, eyes glazed.

Saxon lit a cigarette, walked over and put it in the homicide cop's mouth.

XXIII

IT WAS ONE of the small houses, four hundred seats, small theaters were the only kind that booked him in the big cities any more, and for a magician whose act comprised the entire evening of entertainment, the real magic was any booking at all; even for The Great Saxon, acknowledged not just by press notices and advertisements but other professionals in his trade as the world's foremost sorcerer in the art of legerdemain.

A small, old legitimate playhouse with a dusty-rose, faded brick front on a narrow, cobbled Boston street, the edifice illuminated by glass-enclosed gaslight flickering yellowly, eerily, against the flurry of a softly falling late February snow. It could have been the Eden Theatre in Paris in the 1870s when Hermann the Great performed his Vanity Fair illusion before a dazzling, smartly dressed, properly amazed and appreciative audience that rose applauding wildly when he vanished Mrs. Hermann into her large makeup mirror. Saxon supplied the gaslight torches himself, carrying them with his other props, because that was the aura of illusion he wanted. Those days when magic was revered as great art.

The program announcement posted outside the theater did not proclaim him a magician, that was a common, passé word now: you expected a clumsy clown charade—the man in coattails deliberately bungling simple sleight-of-hand tricks as if by accident to get people to laugh at him. Saxon didn't care to be laughed at. He had even dropped the "Great" from his billing, for it was another old-fashioned cliché. With quiet dignity, the poster read simply:

Tonight at 8: 30
An Evening With
JOSEPH P. SAXON
Performing Supernatural Acts
of Black Magic

That was the only come-on to get an audience. The supernatural. It intrigued people to brave snow and wet streets, paying seven dollars a ticket to witness a master of his craft who (his newspaper write-ups purported) could summon the dead to appear with him on a shabby stage in a tiny, decrepit Boston theater.

And so standing on the last threshold of the once great profession of theatrical legerdemain, using truth for the first time after a thousand lies advanced through three centuries by hundreds of magicians before him, the playhouse was full, a strange, eerie excitement rippling over the audience. His first performance of the season in what was now to be a twenty-week tour of as many cities. And of course in this full house there was the usual sprinkling of skeptics. Up here on stage he could feel their hostility and now and then hear their fanged hissing to one another. But at least they didn't laugh. No one had laughed.

Perhaps because Saxon himself seemed so solemn. As though he believed all he was doing, and they didn't want to spoil it for him. Yet it wasn't really solemnity he felt so much as a nostalgia for a time past when the masters of his craft believed that some day they would become so imbued in the magic to which they were totally devoted that they would eventually, by accident or otherwise, stumble upon dark secrets that would enable them to know and exhibit a true sorcerer's art of supernatural black magic.

He was approaching the finale of his act, his own personal masterpiece, and was downstage now, at the tip of the perimeter, the lights behind him blacked out. His voice was low, conversational. He seemed humble, suddenly unsure of himself. In the soundless hall, the audience had to strain to hear him.

"I was married once. That was a long time ago. It seems eons ago. Though I have learned since there is no such thing as time or space."

He had rapt attention. The soft words seemed addressed not to an audience but you as an individual, and there was something triumphant about Saxon in these closing minutes of the show.

"Those of you who may have read articles about me in one of the news magazines are aware that in the off season from the theater I live an odd and solitary life in an old barn-like apartment on the top floor of a building in San Francisco."

Mingle truth with the Great Truth.

"It is a barren existence but it gives me the solace to meditate . . . and late one night, seated cross-legged in the darkness, holding my mind a blank, playing the worn, old record of a song I had once known in my days with Lida, she slowly appeared before my eyes. I thought I had imagined it, but—"

A gasp from the audience. A soft glow of light was beginning to appear in the darkness behind Saxon. As though unaware of both that and the chilled tension out front, he went on:

"—It was Lida. Since then she has appeared many times—"

Behind him, tiny white dots of light shimmered like a

miniature replica of the snowflakes outside falling past the flickering gaslight. They gradually began to take the form of a woman.

"I wish I could tell you that she will appear again tonight as she has on so many other evenings. But I can't make that promise. She may have been called to a far beyond. And in any case, Lida is very special. She cannot simply be summoned."

An hysterical female voice from the audience called out, *"She's behind you."*

Saxon turned, looked upstage, saw the phosphorous of light slowly flesh out, and "Lida" stood there now: not in the short-skirted garb of the usual magician's assistant. She wore a simple dress, flat-heeled shoes; her tawny blonde hair was pulled back and tied with a green ribbon. She was young, twenty-three, but the audience understood that death knows no age. She had "died" at the age of twenty-three.

There was heavy applause, and when it stopped momentarily, he looked straight at Ellen and said, "Thank you, dear."

Ellen glided toward him, and he embraced her, kissing her on the lips.

Profound, shocked silence out front, then the usual, audible whispers of frightened people who couldn't consciously admit to what they were seeing.

"That's not a ghost. It's a live woman."

"Trick. It's a trick!"

Louder now, not a whisper: "Fake . . . *fake.*"

As if responding to that callous rudeness, Ellen Hayes began to dissolve in Saxon's arms.

Hushed, terrifying silence.

The unexpected.

Suddenly she was gone. Vanished. He stood alone on the empty stage, a hurt look on his face. He gazed out at the audience, then very wearily said:

2

11

"Good night."
The stage blacked out. Wild applause.
But when the lights came up he, too, was gone.
The applause went on but he did not return for a curtain call. He never did.

Let them think the insulting murmur of a few that had frightened "Lida" off cut him so deeply he could not bring himself to come back and bow.

It completed the illusion, that now was no longer illusion, but true, pure magic.